NORTHWOODS SHOOTOUT!

The tall one had turned to say something to his companion when the first shot from one of the windows took him. When the lead tore into him, he reared back in his saddle and started to sag to the ground. Taken completely by surprise, the other swept his hand to his holster. Before he could draw, a second shot barked from the building and he too crumpled, falling forward. The bodies of the two outlaws hit the ground only seconds apart.

Jessie was as completely surprised as the outlaws had been. She made an involuntary effort to move, but her bonds held her motionless. . . .

*   *   *

SPECIAL PREVIEW!
Turn to the back of this book for a sneak-peek excerpt of the new epic western series . . .

THE HORSEMEN

. . . the sprawling, unforgettable story of a family of horse breeders and trainers—from the Civil War South to the Wild West!

Also in the LONE STAR series from Jove

— WESLEY ELLIS —

LONE STAR

IN THE TIMBERLANDS

JOVE BOOKS, NEW YORK

LONE STAR IN THE TIMBERLANDS

A Jove Book / published by arrangement with
the author

PRINTING HISTORY
Jove edition / June 1992

ISBN: 0-515-10866-9

Jove Books are published by The Berkley Publishing Group,
200 Madison Avenue, New York, New York 10016.
The name "JOVE" and the "J" logo
are trademarks belonging to Jove Publications, Inc.

PRINTED IN THE UNITED STATES OF AMERICA

10 9 8 7 6 5 4 3 2 1

LONE STAR

IN THE
TIMBERLANDS

Chapter 1

"Look out, Ki!" Jessie called. "Two of those wolves are trying to sneak up on you! Look behind you! There's one on each side and they're getting dangerously close!"

Ki had just reined his horse around, and when Jessie shouted, he was starting toward her. They'd separated only a few minutes earlier, galloping off in opposite directions when the pack of a dozen or more prairie wolves burst out of the big brush thicket on the Circle Star's outlying range.

Now for the second time in as many minutes Ki yanked at the reins to turn his mount. In his new course he was heading toward the wolf-pack instead of getting out of the way of the leaders of the running and angrily yowling wolf pack.

Even before his mount completed its turn Ki was sliding a *shuriken* from the case on his forearm. He raised his arm the minute he'd gotten the finely honed throwing blade into his hand, and then with a single swift sweep of his arm he launched the wicked steel disk toward the wolf that was leading the pack.

1

In an arc of shining steel the *shuriken* flew to its mark. The razor-sharp blade sliced through the thick fur and leathery skin of the approaching animal's neck. A piercing, protesting yowl of pain broke from the wolf's slavering jaws, but the running animal did not fall.

Instead, it began circling, twisting its head as it tried to reach the steel blade that was embedded in its neck, the blade now dripping blood from the artery it had cut. The wolf had almost reached Ki's horse when it staggered, as Jessie's bullet went home. Its angry yowl of mixed pain and threat faded, then ended suddenly in a final gargling gasp as the animal fell in a crumpled heap.

Jessie's rifle barked again, and another of the advancing wolves stumbled as the slug found its mark. For a moment the big, thickly furred animal lurched from side to side, before dropping in its tracks, where it lay still. Even before the two wolves had fallen, the others in the big pack were closing the circle they'd started to form around Jessie and Ki.

"We'll have to get the lead wolf before this pack gives up," Jessie called to Ki. "But if we can stop them from closing their circle and drop three or four more of them, the rest of them will run."

"I think I've spotted the leader," Ki answered with a nod. He was already drawing another *shuriken* from his case. "It's that big fellow with a light-colored ruff. I'm closer to him than you, but with all the fur in his ruff your bullet will be more effective than my *shuriken*."

"I'll take care of him," Jessie called back.

She returned her attention to the wolf pack. The death of two of their number in such a short time had momentarily slowed their efforts to encircle Jessie and Ki, but had not stopped it. The wolves were getting excited now;

they were snarling more fiercely than before and moving much faster.

Fixing her rifle sights on the big wolf with the light-colored ruff, Jessie triggered off another round. The animal lurched forward and fell, as had the first one she'd shot. It lay twitching for a moment before its final death shudder ended. The wolves remaining in the big pack had not been panicked by Jessie's first shot; nor did her second shot deter them. They kept moving steadily to complete their encircling of the riders.

"It looks like my guess was wrong," Ki called to Jessie. "If that fellow you just brought down had been the leader, these wolves would be running away by now. Have you spotted the pack's leader yet?"

For a moment Jessie did not reply; her attention was still fixed on the wolves. In spite of the deaths of three of their number, the pack had not stopped moving to encircle them.

"It's either that one on my left," Jessie said without twisting in her saddle to face Ki, "the one with the gray-streaked neck fur, or the one nearest you on the right, the one with the dark fur."

"You take the gray-streaked wolf; I'll get the other one," Ki suggested.

He was raising his arm as he spoke, the *shuriken* he'd drawn clasped in his throwing hand. Ki's aim with the third *shuriken* was as accurate as his first throw. The shining, spinning blade took the wolf just above the base of its muzzle, cutting through the thin plate of bone above one eye and slicing into its brain. The animal was lurching forward in the collapse of death when Jessie's rifle barked and the dark-hued wolf that had been her target jerked and fell as her shot went home.

3

It was obvious now to both Jessie and Ki that one of them had brought down the leader of the wolf pack. With five of their number lying sprawled and motionless, the wolves were seized by a sudden panic. They moved aimlessly for a moment, whining in their throats and yapping occasionally, then at top speed they began streaming away from Jessie and Ki.

Ki had no chance to find another target as the wolf pack moved away with such an unexpected speed. Though Jessie squeezed off a final shot, the slug from her Winchester did nothing but raise a puff of prairie dirt between the spread-out forms of the running and now scattering wolf pack. Neither Jessie nor Ki could do anything except watch as the animals streaked away.

Without taking their eyes off the fleeing wolves both Jessie and Ki reined in. Their moves in finding targets had now brought them within easy speaking distance. For a moment they said nothing as they watched the retreating forms of the running wolf pack. Then Jessie turned to Ki.

"It's been a long time since we've had that many wolves in a pack on Circle Star range," she observed. "I can't remember how long it's been since one of the hands had to shoot one, or reported seeing one."

"If I remember rightly, it's been almost two years since the hands had to get rid of a pack of that size," Ki replied. "And we've only had three or four reports of pairs or solitaries in that time."

"That's about what I've been thinking," Jessie said and nodded. "I hope we aren't facing a new wolf invasion. In a way, I really regret having to kill them, but we've got to consider the steers first if we're going to stay in the cattle business."

"There certainly isn't any argument about that," Ki agreed. "My guess is that those wolves have come up here from some new spread to the southeast, where they're just clearing the range and getting it ready to run cattle."

"More than likely," Jessie replied. "And if we're lucky, we won't have a lot of them here on the Circle Star. But I'll tell Greg Dawson to caution the hands about keeping a lookout for wolves from now on."

"Good," Ki nodded. He reined in as they reached the area where the carcasses of the fallen wolves lay scattered. "Let's stop for a minute, Jessie, just long enough for me to get the *shuriken* I had to use."

"Are you getting short of your throwing blades, Ki?" she asked. "If you are, we can get Pablo to make more in his spare time."

"Oh, I've got enough *shuriken* stored away to carry me for a while," Ki said. "It's been a while since I had to use one, except for the old blades I practice with, and I only do that often enough to keep my hand in."

Jessie glanced at the sun, midway between its zenith and the horizon, then said, "We've got plenty of time before dark to finish looking around the rest of this section of range, Ki. We might be a little late for supper, but that's not really important. I'd like to finish looking at this part of the range before we start back to the main house."

"I'm not in any bigger hurry than you are," Ki replied. "And as long as we're out here, we might as well finish the job we came to do."

"I don't suppose we'll be too tired to go over at least part of the quarterly reports after supper," Jessie went on. "They ought to be getting in now. Or we can let the reports wait until tomorrow, and spend our time after

5

supper planning what needs to be done to this section of the range before we add to our cattle herd."

"You're still planning to carry a bigger herd, then?" Ki asked as he returned. When they'd toed their horses into motion, he went on, "It's been at least a month since you said something about using this part of the ranch."

"Perhaps I haven't said much, but I've been doing a lot of thinking. It isn't that I need the money, but you know that I'm very much like Alex in some respects," Jessie told him. "And you know his philosophy. He was never one to give up using land or a factory or mine or any of his other business properties, whatever they happened to be. I'm sure you heard him say that many times."

"You mean his saying that 'what you don't use, you lose'?" Ki asked.

"Exactly," Jessie nodded. "And I've learned that Alex was right about that, just as he was right about so many other things."

"You still miss Alex, don't you, Jessie?" Ki asked. Then he added quickly, "I do, I know, even after all these years."

"I doubt that I'll ever stop missing him, Ki," Jessie said. Her voice was sober as she went on, "Almost every decision I make is influenced by something Alex taught me, or by some chance remark that I heard him make."

Alexander Starbuck, Jessie's father, had been one of America's financial titans. Like so many of the industrial moguls who came into prominence during the years that followed the War Between the States, the young Starbuck had won his fortune by his own efforts, after beginning with a small one-man business. He'd started a curio shop in a ramshackle building on the San Francisco waterfront and in a relatively short period of time had

6

expanded his shop into a sizeable import-export business between the United States and the Orient.

During one of his visits to the Far East in search of merchandise, Alex had encountered Ki. Their chance meeting led to his discovery that Ki was the son of one of Alex's close friends, a naval officer who'd fallen in love with a Japanese girl. Unfortunately, the girl's parents had shut her out of their lives after she'd married Ki's American father, who was an officer in the U.S. Navy on duty in the Orient.

After Ki's parents died in a storm at sea, Ki had grown up on the streets of Japan. As his young manhood approached, he had been unofficially adopted by an aging samurai, a master of martial arts, the indomitable and austere Hirata. After his mentor's death, Ki had moved from one martial arts *do* to another, perfecting his combat skills. Their chance encounter led Alex to offer his old friend's son a job, to go with Alex to America and help him in the operation of his expanding financial and industrial empire.

Ki proved to be an invaluable assistant, relieving Alex of having to remain in the small curio shop and attend to all its petty detail work. While most of the American nation was still recovering from the War Between the States, Alex had been able to expand during the sudden flood of postwar activity.

His first business outside the shop was a major step forward. He'd been able to raise enough cash to buy one of the shipyards that had been built as a wartime necessity and had been offered for sale at a very low price when the war ended. His new operation led to the acquisition of timberlands, to provide the wooden decks, tall masts, and sturdy spars needed by the shipyards.

Branching out from shipping as the nation grew and prospered, Alex expanded into railroads, and then to the steel used in fabricating the rails and locomotives and rolling stock. As his financial position grew in stature and he became more secure, Alex purchased a substantial interest in a major brokerage house and later was able to buy a small, floundering bank that had been founded as a wartime need. The acquisition of other banks followed, and at a relatively early age, Alex Starbuck had become one of America's great tycoons.

Even before Alex had reached his business peak, he'd fallen in love with Jessie's mother and married her. When his beloved new wife died giving birth to Jessie, Alex devoted himself to rearing Jessie into full womanhood. He was helped by a wise old geisha whom Ki had found in San Francisco's expanding Japanese colony.

As Jessie approached young womanhood, Alex enrolled her in one of the exclusive Eastern female academies to complete the somewhat sketchy education he'd been able to give her in the few spare moments of his increasingly busy business life. Alone except for Ki and his business associates, Alex devoted still more time to his expanding industrial empire, while unknown to him a dark cloud was gathering on the horizon of the American business world.

During the years when the War Between the States raged, the industries of America had suffered even as its industrial base expanded in response to wartime needs. With the war's end, industrial America became virtually independent of its European sources for raw materials and factory products. Suffering now for lack of an outlet for their products, a group of European industrialists formed a cartel, which had as its aim the recapture of the United States market by boring from within.

When the cartel's heavy-handed measures found little acceptance in the free atmosphere of American business, its secret operators started relying on force to gain their objective of capturing the bulk of American business. The cartel's masters formed gangs, which were used to intimidate the businesses they wanted, and bit by bit their power grew.

Alex Starbuck was one of the very few men in the United States who recognized and identified the existence of this sinister organization. When his fellow industrialists in the top echelon of the United States business world laughed at his warnings, Alex began to look for a place where Jessie could grow up safely.

Chance in the form of a mortgage forfeiture brought him the ownership of a huge tract of West Texas land. On his first visit to inspect his new acquisition, Alex was impressed by the peaceful isolation and safety that the area promised. He set out to create the Circle Star Ranch on the still largely untamed prairie. After the death of his beloved wife, he made the Circle Star his real home, a place of refuge where Jessie could grow to womanhood.

In one of his few cases of misjudgment, Alex underestimated the tenacity and stealth of the enemies he'd made by opposing the European cartel. While Jessie was still attending her exclusive Eastern boarding school, a murder squad dispatched by the cartel struck the Circle Star. The merciless executioners made a surprise attack, a dozen killers storming the ranch at a time when Alex was riding alone over a section far removed from the main house and the buildings that accommodated the ranch hands. They completed their murderous attack, and Alexander Starbuck died in a hail of the assassins' bullets.

Jessie proved at once that she had inherited her father's determination and courage in addition to learning well the management skills he had taught her. She did not finish her last year at the Eastern boarding school, but insisted that as Alex's only heir she intended to assume the same role her father had played by taking charge of the far-flung industrial and financial empire she'd inherited.

Just as Alex had done before her, Jessie looked on the vast Circle Star Ranch as her true home. In spite of its isolation, or perhaps because of it, she insisted on living in the big ranch house that Alex had planned and built before his untimely death. Though she made mistakes during the early years of managing the many and varied business and financial enterprises Alex had begun, she soon learned to cope with their manifold details by following closely the reports sent quarterly to the ranch by the resident managers.

As Jessie had, Ki also had fallen silent as he recalled the past. Now he said, "I think we'd both be a bit lost if it wasn't for the memories of Alex that we share, Jessie."

"Of course we would," she replied. "And even after so many years, I still find myself trying to think of what Alex would do in some of the situations I encounter."

"Well, neither of us could have a better example to follow in the work we do," Ki said. "And speaking of work, if we're going to finish this inspection job in time to get back to the main house for supper, we'd better keep moving."

Jessie and Ki continued following the quickest route along the Circle Star boundary fence to the rambling ranch house. Even by using all the slanting cutoffs across the open sections of rangeland, the ride back to the main house and its outbuildings was a long one, and darkness caught them before they'd reached their destination.

Jessie was the first to see the distant gleam of lights from the bunkhouse and the cottage occupied by Cliff Peak, the Circle Star's foreman. There were no lights in the cookshack, and only a single window of the big two-story adobe main house cast a yellow gleam through the darkness.

"I'm glad to see that there's a light in the main house," Jessie said. "It means that Gimpy's taken some supper over there for us."

"Yes, and I'll admit I'm getting pretty hungry about now," Ki replied. "Even a cold supper will be a treat."

"If that wolf pack hadn't kept us busy, we'd be getting ready for bed about now," Jessie went on. "But the day's been well spent, Ki. For one thing, we've learned that we're going to have to get rid of that wolf pack before we can turn cattle out on the boundary range."

"It shouldn't take too long to do that, Jessie," Ki told her. "Tomorrow I'll tell Cliff to pick out one of the hands who's a good shot and have him check the range every week or so. Wolves are smart animals, and after two or three of them have been shot, the pack will move on and find a new den."

"Preferably off the Circle Star Range," Jessie said. "And I'll begin to think about either splitting up two or three of our range herds, maybe even buy some fresh stock to put on the range there when it's cleared."

During their brief exchange Jessie and Ki had closed the gap remaining between them and the ranch buildings. They reached the corral and Jessie swung out of her saddle. She looked at the lights in the main house and the foreman's cabin and turned to Ki.

"If you'll take care of the horses, Ki," she said, "I'll stop at Cliff's cabin and tell him what needs to be done. Right now I'm about as hungry as a bear, and

11

I'd imagine that you must be, too. We'll have supper, and after I've eaten it'd take a team of mules to keep me out of bed."

"I feel just about the same way," Ki agreed. "Go ahead, Jessie. I'll join you in just a few minutes."

Jessie started toward the main house, and Ki took up the reins of the horses to lead them into the corral. He checked the feed troughs as quickly as possible before unsaddling the four horses; then, as they started munching, he closed the corral gate behind him and began walking toward the open door of the big main house.

When he stepped inside, he saw Jessie standing at the long table just beyond the door, shuffling through the pile of letters and thickly filled manila envelopes that covered the tabletop. She turned as Ki entered.

"Maybe we should've stayed here and waited for the mail, Ki," she said. "All these quarterly reports seem to have gotten here at the same time, which means we'll be even busier tomorrow than we were today. Let's just leave them where they are. Right at the moment, all I can think of doing is soaking in the bathtub long enough to get rid of the trail dust and then crawling into bed."

Chapter 2

"You must've found something that puzzles you in that report you're reading," Ki observed.

He and Jessie were sitting in the spacious room that had been Alex's study. It was a big room, furnished with comfortable leather-upholstered chairs and and a large sofa in addition to some mementos of her father's beginning days. At opposite ends of the room life-sized oil portraits, one of Jessie's mother, the other of her father, faced each other.

There were still more reminders of Alex Starbuck in the room. Against one wall stood the small, scarred, and battered oaken desk that had been used by Alex in his early days at the crowded waterfront curio shop. Next to the shabby little desk and dwarfing it in size was the large Honduran mahogany rolltop desk from the last office he'd maintained in downtown San Francisco. Ki was always visited by memories when he looked at the small desk, while the larger one brought similar recollections to Jessie.

Ki went on, "For the last quarter of an hour you've

been absorbed in the report on your lap. Is something wrong with it?"

When Jessie failed to reply for the second time, Ki did not repeat his question. Jessie's eyes moved from one to the other of the two oil paintings. One portrayed Jessie's mother soon after her marriage; the other was a study of Alex Starbuck at the height of his career.

Ki knew that Jessie found inspiration—as well as a measure of sadness—in both portraits, and in the moments of leisure that occasionally broke her busy days she would study them in turn. In some mysterious fashion they seemed to inspire her and give her fresh strength to cope with the stresses that went with the busy business life that was her heritage from Alex.

Not wanting to interrupt Jessie's train of thought, Ki began sorting out the reports he'd been going over, arranging them in order of importance for them to discuss later. He'd barely begun his little make-work job when Jessie belatedly replied to his question.

"If you're wondering what's wrong with this report, Ki, it's something I can't put my finger on," she said. "All I'm sure of at this minute is that it's not like any other that I've ever seen from one of my managers."

"Whose report is it?" Ki asked, although he had a very strong hunch that he already knew the answer.

"Jerry Edmonds, at the redwood logging stand in California. And now that I think back a bit, his last quarterly report was a long way from being satisfactory."

"I remember it, too," Ki nodded. "And I found it curious. He'd dropped a long way behind—about ten or twelve percent, as I recall—in the number of board feet of timber the redwood operation is producing."

"It's even worse this quarter, Ki," Jessie went on. "The last quarter showed a six percent decline in the mill's normal production. Now it's dropped to almost ten percent."

"Is Jerry's excuse the same?"

"That's one of the things that bothers me the most, Ki. I know that when I promoted him to be the general manager of the logging stands as well as the mill's operation, our normal production was almost always quite a bit higher than it's been for some time."

"And he doesn't give you any explanation for such a big drop?" Ki frowned.

"Not really," Jessie replied, shaking her head. "The reason he's given this time just doesn't make sense, Ki."

"If I recall his last report he said that he couldn't hire enough timber workers, axmen, and sawyers to handle the redwood stands. And he also mentioned that he couldn't find all the competent mill hands that he needs to turn out finished lumber at the rate that's always been the mill's capacity," Ki went on. "What's his story this time?"

"It's really not new except for one point," Jessie replied. "Other than that he's just repeating the same sort of things he's reported before."

"What's his one point, Jessie? Is there something wrong up in the redwood groves? Some kind of pestilence that's attacked the trees?"

Jessie shook her head and a puzzled frown crept into her face as she replied, "He did mention trouble in the redwood stands, Ki, but then adds something that I don't understand. He says that if the monster would move on, the men would get a lot more work done."

"What monster?" Ki frowned. His frown grew deeper as he went on, "You mean he didn't give you any details? Surely Jerry knows we'd understand something such as wages being too low, good loggers too hard to hire, not enough loggers to fell the trees, not enough mill hands, anything of that sort."

"Of course," Jessie agreed. "Either of us would understand those things. And I'm puzzled about Jerry either being forgetful, or being afraid to give us a detailed report."

"Then what's your answer going to be?"

"I've been trying to decide that ever since I finished going over the report, Ki. Here at the Circle Star there's not any way to find a solution to the problems we're having in the California redwood stands. I'm sure you'll agree with me about that."

"Then what you're saying is that we should get ready for a visit to California?"

"It's the only answer I've been able to come up with, unless you can think of a better way to handle things."

"No," Ki said. "I think you're right, Jessie."

"And something else did occur to me while I've been thinking about our problems in the redwoods," she went on. "That private railroad car that our friend George Pullman has been trying to persuade me to buy has been sitting idle on one of the Circle Star sidings at the station. I can't think of a better way to decide whether or not I want to buy it than using it to make a trip to California."

Ki was silent for a moment; then he said, "I got the idea you were right on the verge of deciding that we'd have to go," Ki said. "As for the private car, I'd almost forgotten it was waiting up at the station for us to use."

"Well, Mr. Pullman told me not to feel obliged to use it right away, so I haven't felt any need to make a special trip."

"Well, I think you're right about using the car on a

long trip. It's certainly the best way to give it a real test," Ki told her. Then he went on, "You've made up your mind about the California trip, then?"

"Unless you can come up with a better idea, Ki."

"I'd be hard put to do that." Ki smiled. "When do you want to leave?"

"There's no point in delaying," Jessie said. "We'll need a day or so to take care of the little odds and ends here that need attention. Since we'll be using the private railroad coach, we'd better send word to the stationmaster and have him arrange for one of the westbound trains to pick it up on whatever day we decide to start."

"That shouldn't be any problem. We can send word to him by the hand who goes to pick up the mail."

"Then all we'll have to do is pack and get to the station stop on time," Jessie said.

"You know, Ki, there's a great deal to be said for travelling in a private car," Jessie observed as she turned away from the big window that dominated the sitting room of the luxurious railroad coach. "And one of the things I wish I'd thought of at the beginning of this trip instead of near the end of it is that we can be doing two things at once. I'd have brought along a few more bits of business paperwork that could stand some extra attention."

They'd been sitting in front of the window as they ate their supper from trays brought in by a smiling porter, watching the landscape that was being taken over by the slowly settling dusk. Late the previous afternoon, as the train topped the gentle rise that marked the southern hills of the Tehachapi Mountains, Jessie had decided on a change in her style of dining. Instead of having the dining-car steward put her dishes on the small table, she'd settled into one of the leather-upholstered easy chairs in front of the window and had the steward rest the tray across the chair's arms.

Ki had liked the idea, and was now sitting in a chair near Jessie's. Like her, he had supported his supper tray on the arms of his chair and was watching the landscape slip by. They'd passed through the verdant San Joaquin Valley now, and the train was chugging along on the peninsula that in a few hours would end at San Francisco.

Ki said, "I like the idea of sitting down to a meal knowing that I don't have to hurry. At suppertime on the ranch there are always some jobs that aren't finished and have left loose ends to be tied up the next day. I like the idea of being able to have our dinner privately, here in the car."

"And I certainly enjoy breakfast on a train much better than I do at the ranch," Jessie went on. "Even if we're used to getting up early."

"But never too early to finish all the chores we've decided to take care of while we were eating supper." Ki smiled. "It seems that we're always hurrying through breakfast because there are a few things we didn't have time to take care of the day before."

"It's lucky that neither of us minds a bit of hurrying, but I must say that time spent on a train is always a pleasant change from our regular routine."

"There's only one thing about being in a private coach that I'm not really fond of," Ki went on. "And that's the lack of exercise. I get a bit stiff when I'm not able to move around."

"There isn't any railroad rule I know of that keeps passengers in their seats all the time, Ki." Jessie smiled.

18

"You can always do a bit of aisle walking and passenger watching. As a matter of fact, I'd like to do a bit of walking myself. Why don't we take an aisle walk together?"

"That's the best idea I've heard all day," Ki said. "We haven't walked entirely through the train since our car was switched to the S.P. tracks at Needles. I don't suppose there'll be a great deal of change, but it'll be interesting to look at the new faces in the passenger coaches."

Putting their supper trays on the floor beside their chairs, Jessie and Ki started their walk toward the front of the train. It was not the leisurely leg-stretching stroll they'd expected, for many of the passengers were no longer sitting passively, gazing from the windows. Almost half of them were beginning to get ready for the moment that was now drawing close, when the train would make its final stop at the Union Station.

Those who had not checked their baggage were in the aisles, lifting valises and suitcases from the luggage racks. Some of the suitcases were both heavy and bulky, and many of the passengers were having trouble getting them down. More often than not, they managed to pull them off the racks only to lose their balance and have the suitcase drag them to one side or the other.

After several occasions when Jessie or Ki barely missed being struck by a suitcase, Jessie turned to Ki.

"This isn't exactly the sort of leisurely stroll along the aisle that I had in mind," she said. "We'll be pulling in there very soon, so suppose we just go back to our car where we can sit peacefully and wait for the train to stop."

"I feel the same way you do, Jessie." Ki nodded. "I see a clear spot in the aisle just a step or two ahead;

we'll have room to turn around there and start back."

Jessie advanced toward the clear spot Ki had indicated and was just stepping into it, getting ready to turn around, when a man bending over a valise on the coach seat lifted his head and turned to glance at her.

"Jessie!" he exclaimed. "Jessica Starbuck! How did we manage to be passengers on the same train without me seeing you?"

"I might ask you the same question, Lee," Jessie replied. "Ki and I started in Texas. But we've been staying in our car most of the time. It's that coach at the rear of the train. Mr. Pullman thinks I ought to buy it from him, so he's loaned it to me for a trial. But I don't know how I could've missed seeing you, wherever you boarded."

"I got on yesterday afternoon, at Bakersfield," he said. "And I certainly did notice the private car, but nobody I talked to seemed to know who was traveling in it." Then, turning to Ki, he went on, "And I'm glad to see you again, too, Ki. I suppose you and Jessie are off on another of your inspection tours, checking up on the Starbuck properties?"

"Something like that." Jessie nodded.

"I hope you plan to stop in San Francisco for a few days," Lee said.

"Just overnight, I'm afraid," Jessie replied. She stopped short as the train ground to a halt.

"Then you and Ki must have dinner with me," Lee suggested. "It's been such a long time since I've seen you, we have quite a lot of catching up to do."

Before Jessie could reply, Ki said, "Suppose you and Jessie have dinner. When I'm in San Francisco, I try to spend any spare time I have visiting my countrymen in Chinatown."

"Jessie?" Lee asked, turning to her. "Does dinner for two appeal to you?"

"Of course," she agreed. "We'll be stopping at the Baldwin House. I'm afraid that Mr. Sharon's Palace Hotel is a bit too big and too fancy for my taste."

"I'll call for you at seven," Lee said. "And we'll spend a pleasant evening talking over what's happened since we were together the last time."

Jessie stopped at the door of her room and turned to face Lee Patterson. She smiled as she said, "I'm sure you didn't think we'd just end our evening with me going into my room and leaving you in the hall, Lee."

"You're quite right, Jessie, though it's been such a long time since we've had a chance to be together I think I was . . . well . . . hoping that you'd invite me in, but a bit concerned that you'd be so tired from traveling that you'd just want to say good-night here in the hall."

"You certainly don't need an invitation," she went on. "Any more than I'd expect one from you."

As she spoke, Jessie was unlocking the door and opening it. She stepped inside and Patterson followed her. The room they entered would have matched a guest room in the home of any of the Golden State's Bonanza Kings. Rich Turkish carpeting covered the floor of the spacious chamber; there were easy chairs near the broad lace-curtained windows that were shielded now by blinds.

Even though the gas was turned low in the elaborate ceiling light, it gleamed from the highly polished bureaus, just as it did from the small tables that were placed conveniently near the lounge chairs, and from the glistening mahogany headboard of the wide bed that dominated one side of the room.

Neither Jessie nor her companion paid any attention to the room's rich furnishings. Jessie turned to Lee Patterson, and he opened his arms to clasp her and pull her close to him. She bent her head back to offer her lips. Patterson covered them with his, and in a moment their tongues entwined in the first lover's kiss they'd exchanged that evening.

As they held their embrace, Patterson began to push down the low neckline of Jessie's off-the-shoulder dress. She helped him in freeing her arms, and before she could wrap them around him again, he'd broken their kiss and was bending to caress her liberated breasts with his lips and tongue. After the long months of her stay on the Circle Star, Jessie was more than ready to enjoy the attentions of a lover.

Freeing an arm from Patterson's embrace, she slid it between them to reach his crotch. The swollen cylinder that greeted her exploring fingers brought to Jessie a small shudder of anticipated delight. She continued to caress him, but now she did not allow the barrier of clothing to come between them. She unloosed his erection and grasped it, but kept one hand free to help him solve the puzzle of small buttons that ran up the back of her frock. Then she shook her shoulders to let her frock as well as her chemise slide down to her waist.

Feeling the moist warmth of Patterson's lips and tongue on her generous breasts and their ruby tips, Jessie joined her lover in the age-old game of undressing one another. Though their movements were a bit clumsy now and then, their aims were soon achieved and Jessie took Patterson's hand to lead him to the bed. They embraced for another long kiss, but now Jessie was clasping him with more than her arms. Her thighs were squeezed together, cradling his rigid shaft in their softness.

Breaking their extended kiss at last, Jessie whispered, "I'm more than ready, Lee. And when I feel what I'm holding between my thighs, I know that you are, too."

As she spoke, Jessie slid her arm between their bodies to place Lee before wrapping her arms around him and pulling him with her as she fell backward onto the yielding mattress.

Lee toppled forward in Jessie's embrace, but he held her close to him to keep from breaking their fleshly bond. Then, as Jessie relaxed the clasp of her thighs, he thrust and she cried out in delight as she felt his swift, firm penetration. They spent a moment getting fully onto the bed without breaking the bond that joined them.

Their lips were still glued together, and for a few moments they lay still, contented to hold their kiss as their writhing tongues entwined. Then Lee began stroking, slowly paced penetrations that brought soft sighs of pleasure from Jessie's throat. The leisurely strokes soon became swift vigorous thrusts, and Jessie started to rotate her hips slowly. Her sighs became panting gasps, and now Lee shortened the intervals between his lusty drives.

Jessie responded by twisting and rotating her hips in tempo with Lee's more forceful thrusts. The tempo of his penetrations increased, and so did Jessie's response. After a few minutes Lee began pounding fiercely, his penetrations deeper and more vigorous. Jessie kept rotating her hips as she passed the moment of self-control and started squirming, her hips rising and falling of their own volition.

For several minutes time seemed to be suspended, and the only noise in the room was the soft thuds that followed each of Lee's vigorous thrusts, and Jessie's sighs of delighted fulfillment. At last they reached the instant of no return. Lee's drives were still lusty and Jessie's response was equally swift.

Then Jessie's throat began to throb with small, ecstatic moans and Lee began a quick trip-hammer pounding that brought the first throbbing cries from her throat. They grew in volume as she met her lover's drives.

Lee faltered once or twice, then succeeded in maintaining the strength of his deep lunges until Jessie cried out in delight as the even tempo of their coupling became a prolonged series of wild bounces. Then Lee lurched forward and lay still as Jessie offered him her lips and they shuddered together through the final seconds of delight, to lie motionless.

Jessie broke the room's silence after several minutes when the only sounds were their gasping inhalations. She said, "We don't really have to move now, Lee. Let's just lie quietly for a few minutes; then we can start again. The best part of the night is still ahead of us, and I expect to enjoy every minute of it."

★

Chapter 3

"That lighthouse on the shore ahead must be Point Arena, Ki," Jessie said. As she nodded toward the rocky shoreline, she put her forefinger down on the map she was holding. "So that means we're getting very close to Mendocino."

She and Ki were standing in the prow of the side-wheel steamboat that was churning through the low, rippling waves of the Pacific Ocean. The sun had already passed across most of the vast expanse of cloudless sky and was dropping toward the distant western horizon. To the east, details of the jagged California coastline were clearly visible, for the side-wheeler's steersman had not changed the straight-line course the ship had been following since they left San Francisco.

Jessie and Ki had been a bit concerned the first time the coastal steamer kept to its steady course as it approached one of the many promontories that jutted from the shoreline. They'd watched across the ship's bow as it drew closer and closer to the menacing stone face of the rocky point of land, and both of them had sighed with relief when the vessel slid by the rising cliff with a good margin to spare.

Later, in a conversation with the deck mate, they'd learned that in most cases the jutting stone spearheads of the shoreline had no relationship to the depth of the water. The mate had added quickly that the ship's navigator not only had a chart on which underwater hazards were shown, but had guided so many vessels along the coastline that all such potential danger spots were stored in his memory.

During the next two days their view of the northern California coast had varied little as the steamer forged ahead, for the shoreline they were passing seemed to repeat itself and the ocean was unchanging. The shore was formed by a series of small bays and river mouths retreating inland between the promontories that extended into the ocean and now and then appeared to reach almost to the ship's course.

From the boat's deck, the shoreline was visible as a mixture of short stretches where the land sloped gently to the water's edge and other expanses where jagged rocky cliffs rose abruptly from the ocean beyond an expanse of white-capped water. Between ship and shore the ocean's surface was broken here and there into narrow splashes of white spray by the tops of underwater rock formations that rose above the rippling waves.

Where the water receded into bays there was little detail visible, and even when the shoreline jutted into the ocean in sweeping points, the only details that Jessie and Ki could see on the land were an occasional high, jagged rock formation and, at the end of the first day, the stumps of big redwood trees that had been cut in earlier days. However, where the shoreline curved inward to form a cove or bay, the shore was often visible only as a dark line between the surface of the ocean and the sky.

"We still have quite a way to go," Ki remarked, looking up from the map he'd been consulting. "It's been such a long time since we've traveled up here by boat, I've almost forgotten the landmarks."

"Unless my memory's gone back on me, I certainly can't see that it's changed much," Jessie went on. "But you're right, Ki. It has been several years since we looked at the shoreline from the ocean."

"Four years at least, perhaps five," Ki agreed. "Trains today are so much faster than ships. They're more convenient in other ways, too."

"But you know, I'm really glad we decided to come up here on a ship this time, Ki," Jessie continued. "The redwoods are so imposing when you're in one of the forests, and then you're so close to them that they make you feel insignificant. But when you look at them from a distance, the way we are now, you're still impressed, but not really overwhelmed."

"I'm sure we'll have plenty of chances to be overwhelmed when we get inland to the logging stands," Ki went on.

"Yes," Jessie agreed. Then she added, "And after the type of reports we've been getting from Jerry Edmonds, I hope that seeing the operation for ourselves will give us a better idea of the kind of problems he's been facing. But until we do get there, I intend just to relax and enjoy our little voyage."

"I'm sorry we had to delay supper so long, Ki," Jessie said when she had changed her clothes. She and Ki were walking down the deserted corridor of the hotel's ground floor, on their way to the restaurant. "But I certainly didn't expect to be soaked to the skin in that small boat we had to use to get to shore."

"Don't worry," Ki told her. "I'm really not hungry enough for a little delay to bother me. But after three days of ship's food, I'm sure that I'll do justice to whatever's on the menu."

"Well, I'm hungry enough to want a really good-sized meal," Jessie admitted. "Having an unplanned shower bath out in the Pacific Ocean seems to have whetted my appetite."

"I can't understand why the people here in Mendocino don't improve their harbor," Ki said and frowned. "There's certainly enough lumber being shipped out to justify building a harbor where the lumber barges and freighters can load. But I suppose most of the lumber mills here are like yours; they have their own little harbors where the flatboats can put in to get their cargoes."

"And perhaps they hate to change old established ways," Jessie suggested. "But I certainly didn't realize that I was going to be soaked to the skin in the little distance between the ship and the harbor, if it can be called a harbor."

"It's lucky we'd arranged to stay at the hotel," Ki went on. "If we'd been staying at the mill, we'd still be on our way there, and you'd be frozen in that cold wind that always seems to be blowing off the ocean." He was also soaked.

"It's going to be a bit strange, staying here in the hotel instead of going right out to the mill and moving into the guest cabin, as we usually do," Jessie went on. "But I want this visit to be a surprise. If we'd intended to stay at the mill, I'd have needed to notify Jerry Edmonds that we were planning to be here."

During their brief exchange, Jessie and Ki had kept moving steadily down the stairs. The hotel's lobby was narrow and cramped, and they passed through it quickly, heading for the dining room. When they entered it, neither Jessie nor Ki was surprised to see that, in addition to tables spaced about the big room, one of its rear corners was devoted to an L-shaped bar, where a cluster of men stood with drinks in their hands or in front of them on the polished mahogany.

Absorbed in conversations, the drinkers paid no attention to the restaurant area, where only three of the dozen or so tables were occupied. The bartender was obviously as interested in the verbal exchanges between the drinkers as were the men on the opposite side of the bar.

"I suppose we just choose one of the tables and sit down to wait until somebody shows up to take our orders," Jessie said.

"Of course," Ki replied. "In a town this small, I'm sure there's not a restaurant where you'd see a maître d'hôtel."

"Then let's take that table over by the wall," she went on. "It's standing there all by itself, so we'll be able to talk about our plans without anyone overhearing us."

They settled down at the table Jessie had indicated and glanced around, looking for a waiter. When they failed to see one, Ki said, "There doesn't seem to be any service here, except at the bar. I wonder if we're supposed to go to the barkeep—or even to the kitchen—and give our orders for dinner."

"Oh, I'm sure that even in a town this small a restaurant that's in a hotel will have some kind of service," Jessie replied. "Mendocino's off the beaten track, and it's a small town, but even as isolated as it is, whoever runs the hotel must surely know enough to have a waiter or two."

"I think what we're going to find is that the waiter is also the bartender," Ki said. He tilted his head slightly to indicate the bar.

Jessie looked in the direction of Ki's almost imperceptible nod and saw that the aproned barkeeper had left his post and was moving toward their table. He stopped when he reached them and bobbed his head.

"Sorry if I kept you folks waiting," he said. He was scanning their faces with a slight frown, as though trying to recall their names, or deciding whether he'd seen them before. He went on, "I was sorta busy, yarning with the fellows, and just didn't look around much."

"I don't suppose the waiting's really hurt us," Jessie told him. "But right at the moment we're a bit anxious to eat our dinner. You are here to take our orders, aren't you?"

"I sure am, ma'am," he replied. "Strangers in town, ain't you? Because I sure don't remember seeing you in here before now."

"We're not exactly strangers," Jessie said. "But we don't come here very often, and usually when we do we stay at the Starbuck Mill, which I happen to own. If you'd care to step out to the desk, you'll find that we're registered as guests here in the hotel. I'm Jessica Starbuck, and this gentleman is Ki, my special assistant."

"Well, bless me from Dan to Beersheba and back!" the man exclaimed. "I've heard young Jerry Edmonds say your names every now and then, when he comes in, but I never did have nobody to fit faces to 'em. I'm Edgar Hewlett, ma'am. Folks call me Ed whether or not they know me. I been trying to run this place the right kinda way ever since I bought it three or four years back, but it gets pretty hard sometimes. Town's not growing any bigger, and maybe it's even going down a bit. Keeping a place like this is a job any way you wanta look at it, but I'm managing to hold on."

"I'm glad to hear that you are," Jessie said. "But we're really very hungry. Can't we start our dinner now, and visit later?"

"Why, sure!" Hewlett replied. "All I got to do is tell the cook to dish up your grub, and that won't take but a minute. I'll hustle on back to the kitchen right now, and get Cookie busy fixing up your plates. He'll bring 'em out here to you."

As Hewlett took their orders and left, Jessie smiled at Ki and said, "Nobody could accuse Mr. Hewlett of being unfriendly."

"Or uncommunicative, either," Ki agreed. "But I don't think we can blame him for being something of a chatterbox. He must be having a pretty tough time keeping this place going, if you judge by the number of customers he has in here right now."

"Well, about all that we can do is wish him luck," Jessie said. "But I see that he's coming out of the kitchen now, so we should be getting our dinner fairly soon."

"It can't get here too soon to please me," Ki told her. "And by the time we've finished eating I'm sure we'll both be ready to get into the kind of beds that don't try to throw you out when a ship lurches around."

"It certainly wasn't the most restful night I've spent, and it has been a busy day," Jessie agreed. "But we'll be staying here long enough to get rested before we go on with our trip. Then we'll be in the carriage for the trip to the mill, so we know we'll be comfortable."

Ki had been glancing around the big room as Jessie spoke. Now he said, "Our host must be telling his friends who we are, Jessie. All of them are glancing our way, and none of them are trying to hide their curiosity."

Jessie turned her head the small distance needed for her to get a clear view of the group at the bar. All but one of them turned away when they saw her looking at them. The man who was the exception made some quick remark to his companions; then he broke away from the bar and started toward the table where Jessie and Ki were sitting.

Keeping her voice to a half-whisper, she said, "It looks as though we're about to have a visitor, Ki. And unless I'm mistaken, he's one of the sawmill operators that we've been introduced to on one of our trips here. I can't remember whether it was a year or two years ago, and I can't recall his name right now, but I'm sure we've met him before."

"You're right," Ki agreed. "I recognize him now. And—" He broke off as the approaching man got within easy earshot of their table.

"I reckon I'd best apologize for busting in on you and your friend, Miss Starbuck," he said. There was no hint of an apology in his voice. "You might recall that we got introduced when you was here about two years or so ago. In case you've forgot, I'm Vance Harper."

"I do remember meeting you, Mr. Harper," Jessie said. "And you'll remember Ki, because he's been with me on every visit I've made here."

Harper nodded in Ki's general direction, then turned back to Jessie. "I don't mean to take your mind off of your supper," he went on. "And I'll make myself scarce soon as they get it here from the kitchen."

"You're not disturbing us at all," Jessie said. "It's thoughtful of you to stop and say hello to us."

"I come over here to say a little bit more than just hello," Harper told her. "Except that I don't reckon this is the best time to say it."

"Perhaps if you just give me an idea, we can sit down later on and talk," Jessie suggested.

Harper did not reply for a moment; then he said, "I don't play my cards close to my vest when I'm in a poker game, Miss Starbuck. When all the chips are on the table I lay my cards down faceup, and I do the same thing when I'm making a business deal."

"I've played a little poker myself, Mr. Harper," Jessie replied levelly. "But I prefer to look at my cards carefully before I bet on a hand."

"Well, I guess all of us do business in our own way," Harper said. "But I'll show you my hand right now."

"Please do." Jessie nodded.

Nodding, Harper went on, "I want to buy whatever you've got up here in the Mendocino country. And I mean it when I say I want everything. That'd take in all your timber stands, whether you own them or lease them. It'd include standing sales contracts, your sawmills and all your other machinery, haulage contracts, hands' houses, boats, whatever it might be."

Harper's offer was so totally unexpected that Jessie was taken off-guard. However, she'd been in similar situations often enough to realize that replying to him immediately would be a mistake. Jessie allowed no expression to show on her face or in her actions and avoided any movement that might give Harper a hint of her reaction before she replied to his surprising offer.

When Jessie finally spoke, her voice was as politely level as though she were turning down an invitation to have a cup of tea. She said, "I'm not at all interested in selling any of the Starbuck properties, Mr. Harper.

33

Even if I had a mind to sell the redwood stands I own along this section of the coast, I'm afraid that any price I'd have to put on them would be out of your reach."

"Don't sell me short, ma'am," Harper shot back. "If I didn't have the money, I'm sure ready to get it quick. You ask around. You'll find out that I can come up with enough to buy you out twice over."

"Without any evidence that you can, I suppose you'll expect me to take your word for that," Jessie said thoughtfully. "But I'm sure you wouldn't offer a deal such as you've just proposed unless you were prepared to follow through with it."

"Try me and see," Harper's tone was challenging. "Once we sit down to work out a price, the money'll be ready."

"You're getting a bit ahead of yourself," Jessie told him. Her voice was cold now. "I've given you my answer, and I don't change my mind about such matters."

"You might take a different look at how much you'd be making after we get down to brass tacks about the cold hard cash I'm ready to put on the line."

Shaking her head, Jessie said, "You're very persistent, Mr. Harper. I'll give you that much credit. But my lack of interest in selling any of the Starbuck properties isn't confined to the ones here in the Mendocino country. My answer's just the same as it would be if you were offering to buy one of the banks or a brokerage office or . . . well, I don't think I care to go any further with this line of conversation."

"Oh, I know you're rich as all get-out, Miss Starbuck," Harper said. "But a lady like you, that's had a lot of experience in business oughta know that whatever timberland you own up here right now won't be worth anything much after all the redwood trees have been chopped down and milled into boards."

"That won't be for many years," she said quietly. "And the way America's growing, there'll be other kinds of work that will give jobs to men who're now cutting trees in the redwoods."

"I've heard that said before," Harper snorted. "But a redwood tree takes a long time to get of a size that keeps a lumber mill in business."

Before Jessie could reply, a waiter arrived with a laden tray. Jessie and Ki leaned away from the table while he transferred their food from his tray. Then before Harper could pick up their conversation again, Jessie spoke.

"I'm afraid there isn't much point in going on with our conversation, Mr. Harper," she said. "You've made your offer and I've refused it. No matter how many times you repeat it, my answer will be the same. Now, if you'll excuse us, Ki and I would like to eat our dinner before our food gets too cold."

For a moment it appeared that Harper was going to persist in his offer. Then when he broke the silence, the anger that had tinged his voice had vanished.

"I'm sorry if I've upset your supper, Miss Starbuck," he said. "You see, I've been figuring for a long time that I might make a deal with you, and putting money aside for it. I won't say I'm mad because you told me no, but don't expect me to stop offering."

"You're very persistent, I must say," Jessie replied, trying to smile in order to diminish Harper's anger at her continued refusal. "But I'll tell you once more that I have no interest at all in selling. And as I've already said several times, I'm not going to change my mind."

"Sure." Harper nodded. "But that's exactly what I'm figuring you just might do after you've had time to take

35

a good look around the redwood stands and see what's going on. Now, I'll say good evening and leave you to your supper."

Harper turned and started back to the bar. Jessie waited until she was sure he was out of earshot; then she said to Ki, "I didn't particularly care for Mr. Harper's style. Did you, Ki?"

"Of course not. But I don't suppose he's able to change it. From the first minute when he made his offer, I've been wondering why he made it and how he was going to make good on it. Your holdings up here are simply too big a bundle for him to manage, Jessie."

"That's what I've been thinking, too, Ki." She nodded. "Although I don't believe he was lying when he hinted that he has some men behind him who're ready to come up with the cash he'd need to swing the deal he offered. But that's not important. I'm starving, and our supper's getting cold. Let's eat and call it a day. We'll wait and see what happens next."

Chapter 4

"I'm really sorry that before you started from Texas you didn't send word you were planning to come up here for a visit, Jessie," Jerry Edmonds said.

"You should've learned by now that I have a pretty good reason for everything I do," Jessie replied.

She, Ki, and Edmonds were in the room—more cubbyhole than office—of the mill manager. Jessie and Ki had just arrived. They'd left the hotel after breakfast and made the short trip to the mill in the town's only closed carriage, a chariot coach that had seen far better days.

"And your reason this time was to surprise me by coming to Mendocino without letting me know?" Edmonds asked. His voice showed a tinge of anger as well as puzzlement as he went on. "I know my quarterly report wasn't too good, but it's not from lack of trying."

"I can understand business slumps, Jerry," Jessie said. "But I get worried a bit when two quarterly reports in succession show such a drop in production as yours have. I like to look at things myself and try to help if

37

I can. I'm sorry if I gave you the impression that I was trying to sneak up on you."

Almost before Jessie paused, Edmonds said, "I'm certainly not objecting to a surprise visit, Jessie. But I wish you'd let me know right away when you got off the ship. I'd have had the guest quarters here at the mill ready for you to step into them and be at home."

"I had good reasons for waiting until this morning to let you know Ki and I were here," Jessie told him. "Suppose you think a minute and then tell me what you'd've done if you'd known in advance that I was coming to visit the mill."

Edmonds did not wait the minute Jessie had suggested before replying, "I'd've certainly tidied things up a bit. And I'd've had the guest house ready for you. You wouldn't have had to wait to move into it."

"That's the exact point I'm making." Jessie smiled. "You can surely understand that I was curious to see how the mill and the loggers were doing in everyday routine work without being warned that I was going to be here."

"Oh, now, Jessie!" Edmonds protested. "You're making it sound as though I'd have staged some kind of show to impress you if I'd known of your visit in advance."

"No, I don't think you'd have gone that far, Jerry. But I knew I'd arrive before a letter could reach you, and if I'd sent you a message over Mr. Morse's telegraph, it would have gotten here several days before Ki and I did. You'd have put in those days preparing for my visit. I'm sure you'd have had the mill hands tidying up and getting everything swept and wiped and polished."

Edmonds was silent for a moment; then he managed a little lopsided smile and said, "I guess you knew that

I couldn't've resisted doing that, Jessie. But I don't see anything wrong about wanting to put my best foot forward."

"There isn't anything wrong with it," Jessie assured him. "But I don't expect—and never did expect—to see a sawmill that doesn't have a lot of sawdust and bark and litter on the floor and in the corners. It certainly won't make me the smallest bit unhappy."

"Well, you're not going to see the mill as littered up as it is when we're running at full production speed," Edmonds said. "And that isn't because I don't run the mill at full capacity a good part of the time. It's because the timber scouts and the woods crews have had some problems."

"Even if you didn't mention problems in your quarterly report, I could read between the lines and get the impression that you've run into difficulties, Jerry," she said.

"But I wasn't trying to hide them," he protested. "I just didn't want to emphasize them."

Before he could say anything more, Jessie went on, "I'm certainly not suggesting you were trying to hide anything. I understand that what you wanted to do was make your report look good. But figures don't lie unless they're twisted, and I'll give you full credit for not doing that."

"But I still don't exactly come out smelling like a rose."

"Let's put off any more talk about your figures until I've had a chance to look around," Jessie suggested. "My main interest is the mill's output. I like to see it hold to a level. Of course, the market for lumber dips now and then, but wood's easy to store even for a long time, and it's there to sell when the demand increases."

"And we'll have plenty when the time comes," Edmonds said, a touch of bitterness in his voice.

"So much the better," Jessie told him. "What concerns me is why the mill's output has dropped. You're working the same number of men that you generally do, give or take a half-dozen, so when I went over the report's figures and saw how much we've dropped in production, I got very curious to find out why. Suppose you tell me now. Is there a gang of timber pirates at work again? I know we've had trouble with them several times in the past."

"And I'm sure we'll have more trouble in the future," he said. "There are some very strange things happening in the redwood stands, Jessie."

"Strange in what way?" She frowned. "Just on the surface, I can't imagine what they might be. The mill's the first place where I'd look for trouble. Quite some time ago, before I put you in charge, there was talk of some mill workers going out on a strike, but that blew over in a very short time."

"I haven't heard any hints that the mill workers might be trying to organize a union." Edmonds frowned. "They've tried twice now, but they can't get enough men to join."

"Is the new owner of the other mill trying to make trouble for us, then?" Jessie asked. "The way they did once before, lurking in the brush and taking potshots at the lumberjacks while they're working the redwood stands?"

Edmonds shook his head. "No. It's the felling crews out on the timber stands that aren't doing their jobs. We've had to cut back on manpower and working hours here at the mill because we're not getting enough trees."

"And you don't have any reason why?" Ki put in.

"I suppose I could give you both a yes and a no for an answer, Ki," Edmonds replied. "Or I could just say the Mendocino Monster."

"And what does that mean?" Ki asked.

Smiling as he spoke, Edmonds replied with a question of his own. "You mean that you've never heard of the Mendocino Monster?"

"No, but I'm sure there are a lot of things in the world that I've never heard of," Ki went on. "Though I've been told of the Loch Ness Monster, and I've heard my own countrymen talk about their ancestors seeing dragons."

"I've never heard of the Mendocino Monster, either," Jessie said. "Just exactly what are you talking about, Jerry?"

"Maybe you haven't heard about him because the folks hereabouts sort of fight shy of doing much talking about him," Edmonds replied. "But if you can go by the way they describe him when they do talk, he's a giant that's hairy like a bear. Oh, yes, he's supposed to walk like a man and has unusually large feet, too."

"If he looks like a bear, perhaps he is one," Jessie suggested.

"That's possible, of course," Edmonds agreed. "But there are enough bears—blacks and a few grizzlies— wandering in the redwoods for anyone who knows the country to tell the difference between him and a bear."

"I'd suppose there are quite a lot of people who can't make the distinction, though," Jessie said thoughtfully.

"And let's not forget what imagination does," Ki suggested. "It might be nothing more than a shadow in the night or the result of somebody's dreams."

"Plenty of people here in Mendocino think almost exactly as you do, Ki," Edmonds nodded. "But there are just as many others who swear that whatever this monster is, it has hands and feet like a man and a face like a man, but is too big to be a man. I've never seen him myself, but there are a lot of lumberjacks who swear they have. All I've seen of him are some unusually big footprints that everybody here in Mendocino swears are his."

"Is he—or maybe I ought to say 'it'—supposed to be dangerous?" Ki frowned.

"Yes, 'it' might be a better word," Edmonds said. "About half the people who claim to've seen it can't answer that question without getting into an argument. But I go on the assumption that if it really is dangerous, and kills everybody it can run down, there wouldn't be any survivors to tell their stories."

"Has anyone ever seen the body of a person this thing is supposed to've killed?" Jessie asked. "Or does anybody claim to have faced him and fought with him?"

"Not to my knowledge," Edmonds replied. "But quite a few people do disappear from this part of the Mendocino coast. They just drop out of sight and aren't seen again."

"But people disappear for all sorts of reasons," Jessie objected. "Anyhow, whether it's real or not, we'll be on the lookout for your monster, Jerry, though I doubt we'll see it. But what I started to say a minute ago is that I do want to spend some time in the redwoods while we're here. Alex taught me to love the big trees, even if he did buy this mill to cut them into boards."

"Something's just occurred to me," Ki said. "Isn't it possible that some of the lumberjacks started this story as a joke, and after people talked about it for a while, it began to be accepted as real?"

"Of course it's possible," Edmonds agreed.

"That's what I've been thinking, too," Jessie put in. "Having a mysterious monster to fall back on for an

42

excuse would certainly be an easy way to cover up a lot of vandalism, even murder."

"Except for the disappearances, I've never heard of the monster being blamed for anything except frightening somebody," Edmonds said. "Which isn't quite the same as using him as an excuse to account for a mistake, or for reporting late for a work shift. Or to cover up vandalizing another sawmill's gear."

Jessie turned to Ki and said, "I can't remember that we've had trouble of that sort. And we've always gotten along quite well with the other mills along the Mendocino coast. Ki, you came here several times with Alex. Do you recall him making any enemies here?"

Ki shook his head. "No. Your father had the knack of getting along with even his keenest competitors."

Jessie turned to Jerry Edmonds and asked, "What about this new mill operator, the one who also owns the hotel? Do you get along with him?"

"We're not what you'd call close friends, but we've never been at odds with one another," the mill superintendant answered. "Another problem is that we contract the tree felling and strip cutting and hauling to that outfit over in Indian Creek, so the timber crews don't come here to the mill very often."

"Then you don't know them well?" Ki asked.

"I don't see them often enough. They stay at their camps out in the groves. I've certainly tried to do my best in keeping on good terms with them, of course."

Jessie had been standing silently thoughtful during the exchange between Ki and Edmonds. Now she said, "Well, at least we've gotten down to the bottleneck. This is as good a time as any to see if we can't open it up."

"What do you have in mind, Jessie?" Edmonds asked.

43

"Since the first time Alex brought me here as a little girl, I've been fascinated by the redwoods," Jessie replied. "It's been a long time since I've seen them, though. Now that Ki and I are here, I'd not only like to visit the other mills hereabouts, I'd like to combine my trip inland with a visit to the groves."

"Perhaps you hadn't noticed it, Jerry, but Jessie likes to combine business with pleasure when it's practical," Ki said, smiling as he spoke.

"Well, I can't see anything wrong with that, Ki," Jessie said before Edmonds could answer. "It'll just mean a few little side trips while we're looking over the logging camps. I'll have a chance to watch the lumberjacks at work, and talk to whoever's in charge of them. Perhaps they just need a little bit of pushing. If they don't take it kindly, they'll blame us instead of Jerry."

"Now, Jessie, I'm here to do the pushing and take the blame as well," Jerry put in. "But if you don't want me tagging along with you—"

"It's not that, Jerry," Jessie broke in. "What I'm thinking of is that you have to deal with the loggers regularly. Ki and I are new faces."

"Jessie's right, you know," Ki said quickly. "We can poke around and ask questions which the loggers might resent a bit from you because you're supposed to know the answers. We're not, and when we get back we can go over with you the things we've been told. You can tell us very quickly whether we were answered truthfully or just told a bunch of lies."

"That does make sense." Edmonds nodded. "When do you want to go, Jessie?"

"It seems to me that right now is the best time we'll have," Jessie replied. "We'll talk about the mill when Ki and I get back. "We can rent horses and saddle gear here in Mendocino, right?"

"Oh, of course," Edmonds replied. "There are two livery stables in town. I don't think there were any the last time you were up here."

"Yes, I remember quite well. We had to ride mill horses that were more accustomed to pulling lumber wagons than having riders on their backs." Jessie nodded. Turning to Ki, she went on, "We'll travel light, just take enough supplies for a several days or so. Who knows? You and I might run into the monster ourselves."

Jessie looked at the roiling surface of the river as it tossed in streaks of greenish white foam. Here and there the froth of conflicting currents broke the patternless surface to form big bubbles that appeared for a shining moment before being swallowed by the rushing stream.

"It doesn't seem as if we'll ever find a place that looks safe to wade the horses across, Ki," Jessie said. "Maybe we'd better turn back and cross at that one spot we passed where we could see bottom."

"We've come quite a way since then," Ki replied. "And if we turn back to the place you're talking about it'll be dark before we get there."

After a glance at the sun, hanging only a hand span above the western horizon, Jessie nodded agreement. She said, "Well, as much as I'd like to get to those trees on the other side of the river, I suppose you're right. I certainly wouldn't want to try crossing at any of those shallow places we've already passed, but we'll have to get across sooner or later."

"Let's move ahead, then," Ki suggested. "There's bound to be some place ahead where we'll find a stretch of calm, shallow water. If we don't run across one before dark, we'll just have to pick out the best spot we can find to spend the night."

"It wouldn't be the first time we've made a rough camp," Jessie went on. "And we'll certainly be better off moving ahead than we would staying here."

Toeing their mounts ahead, Jessie and Ki continued moving along the riverbank, scanning the landscape ahead in search of some spot where they could spread their blankets for the night. The sun was dropping below the horizon before they found what they were looking for—a notch in the low, gently up-slanting side of the riverbed.

Jessie reined in and Ki brought his horse to a halt beside her. Indicating the little arroyo, she said, "I suppose this is the best spot we'll find before it's too dark to see anything."

The small expanse was covered with a scant growth of struggling grass blades trying to thrive on the ocher-colored earth. The arroyo was not large; it was only a small arc of green in the seemingly endless gray-white stony soil.

"Let's make camp here and call it a day," Jessie said.

"I'm as ready as you are," Ki agreed. "I'll help you get our blankets spread. Then while you're getting whatever we have to eat out of our saddlebags, I'll take the horses down to drink and fill our water bags."

Veterans at making a quick camp, Jessie and Ki spent little time in their preparations for the night. They munched their pickup supper in silence while watching the cloudless sky's transition from dusk to darkness. As the sky's blue deepened into a velvety black and the stars appeared, they sought their bedrolls and stretched out, ready for sleep.

It was the dark phase of the moon, and only the faint susurrus of the river's ever-changing and small, almost whispering bubbling broke the little vale's stillness. Within a few minutes both Jessie and Ki were sleeping soundly. Neither of them stirred as the night slipped past the midnight hour. Slumber still held them when the dark, night-shielded hulking form moved soundlessly along the riverbank and stopped at the water's edge to stand and peer through the gloom at the blotched rectangles of the two bedrolls.

For several moments the hulking figure remained motionless. Then it moved again, slowly and carefully, so silently that it appeared to be a nimbus just a bit lighter in hue than the darkness itself. In its cautious advance toward Jessie and Ki the moving figure made no noise except for the occasional slight tick of rock scraping against sandy soil.

The moving figure could not move with total silence; nor could it see the few faint streaks of rocky threads in the earth. It had covered almost half the distance to the spot where Jessie and Ki were sleeping when its advancing foot landed and grated on an invisible sand-covered streak of loose stones.

This time the noise—slight as it was—reached Ki's ears. Always a light sleeper, he was halfway awakened by the tick, no louder than the sound of a landing sparrow. Ki stirred as he wakened, but did not move. Instead, he strained his hearing, wanting to be sure that he had not just imagined the faint sound.

Though the time that passed between his coming fully awake and the moment when the advancing figure moved forward another step was very short indeed, Ki had begun to strain his eyes, trying to look through the

47

darkness. At last he saw the black hulk of the intruder outlined against the stars.

Now he moved swiftly and surely. He slid a *shuriken* from its leather carrying case and held it, his fingers tight and in the throwing position. Still lying prone, he sent the razor-edged throwing blade on its way.

★

Chapter 5

Visible only as a thin streak against the night sky, Ki's *shuriken* whirled to its target. Though he had not thrown it blindly, the darkness had made accurate aiming almost impossible, and the blade barely touched the end of the intruder's shoulder. Small as the *shuriken*'s impact and bite had been, the shadowed figure outlined against the stars loosed a puffing grunt of pain. Then Ki saw the interloper whirl with incredible quickness and start to run away.

Before the running figure could cover enough distance to be hidden by the darkness, Ki was already moving in pursuit. He'd covered only a few yards when he realized that the mysterious night visitor had reached full speed and was outdistancing him. However, he could still see the shadowy fleeing form.

Ki had already taken a second *shuriken* from its case. He held it poised, trying to gauge his throw, but even his keen eyes could not penetrate the night's blackness well enough to give him a positive target. The vague outline of whoever or whatever Ki was chasing was now almost completely invisible. The scuffing of running feet and the occasional spattering of loose gravel were becoming his only clue to guide him in giving chase.

After a few seconds even these faint noises diminished and vanished. Ki stopped to make it easier for him to see and hear, but the night was now silent, and he could not detect any sign of movement. For a moment he considered continuing his pursuit of the unknown visitor, but then he realized that this would be futile. He was still standing and weighing the options that now remained to him when Jessie broke the silence.

"Ki?" she called. "Did a noise wake me up, or did I—"

"There were some noises, but I didn't make them," Ki broke in. "But everything's calm now." Jessie's question was enough to start him moving back to the spot where they'd bedded down, and as he moved he went on. "Somebody was trying to sneak up on us. I guess it'd be more accurate to say that they did sneak up on us, but when they moved around they made enough noise to wake me up."

"Did you see whoever it was?"

Ki shook his head as he said, "It was too dark for me to see much of anything except a blob in the night. I threw a *shuriken*, but it must've missed, though I could almost swear I heard whoever it was grunting right after I'd let my blade loose. I didn't get a chance to throw another one; before I could get it out of my case whoever it was had started running away."

"You're assuming it was a man? Not a bear or some other kind of animal?"

"From the quick glimpse I got I'd be inclined to say it was either a man or a bear."

"Then you really didn't get a good look?" Jessie asked as Ki reached her side.

He shook his head, then went on. "No. I just got a very blurred glimpse of a blackish form against the stars. For all I know, it could've been some logger on his way to or from town. I'm not at all sure who or what it was, maybe a man, maybe a bear. All that I'm actually sure about is that there was somebody or something poking around our bedrolls. It might even have been the mysterious Mendocino Monster that Jerry was telling us about."

"If there really is such a thing as the monster," Jessie said. "I'm not sure I'll believe there is such a creature until I see it or him, whichever it might be. For the time being, let's just assume it was a man. But whoever or whatever this prowler was, Ki, you don't have any idea what he might look like?"

Ki shook his head as he replied, "Not the slightest. I'm half-guessing even when I say that I got the impression that he was big. I only saw him for a few seconds."

"He didn't say anything, then?"

"Just that grunt I thought I heard," Ki told her. "And then he turned and started running."

"And you didn't try to chase him?"

"I tried, but the noise died away before I could really get started. I don't hear a thing now."

"Neither do I," Jessie agreed. "But even when I woke up I didn't hear any kind of noise that I can remember."

"He had a heavy footstep, Jessie," Ki said, "but he'd gone by the time you woke up."

"From what you've told me, I don't imagine you'd've been able to catch him even if you could've kept within earshot of him." Jessie frowned as she spoke. Then she went on, "For all we know it might've been some roaming lumberjack heading to town, or just shifting from one logging camp to another."

"Well, whoever it was is long gone by now," Ki said. "But when daylight gets here we'll look around and see if we can find any footprints."

"How long do you suppose it is until daylight, Ki?"

"I couldn't even begin to guess. If we were back at the Circle Star, I could get a pretty good idea by looking at the star patterns, but they're too different here."

"Yes," she agreed. "I glanced up a minute or so ago and realized that."

"Right now, I haven't had all the sleep I'd like to get," Ki went on. "Do you think that between now and daybreak we ought to take turns sleeping, one of us staying up in case our uninvited guest comes back?"

"If you can call him a guest, and whoever or whatever it was should come back, it'd be thoughtful if one of us was awake to welcome him," Jessie replied. "But I doubt that he'll make another visit. I'd say let's both turn in again and finish out the night. If we don't get enough rest, we'll pay for it tomorrow. Or today, since it must be well past midnight by now."

"That'd be my idea, too, Jessie," Ki agreed. "And he may have left a trail we can follow by daylight. Though I don't know that catching him would be worth the effort."

They huddled into their bedrolls again. Even though they were several miles inland, the chilling wind from the ocean was still cold enough to make the night air uncomfortable. Within a few minutes after they'd burrowed into their bedding both Jessie and Ki were sleeping soundly again.

• • •

"I think we might as well stop looking, Ki," Jessie suggested. They'd circled twice around the spot where their bedrolls were spread, but even in the day's beginning light they'd seen nothing that gave them a clue. She went on, "If our visitor had left any footprints last night, we'd surely have seen them. I did see a few scuffed places in what little soft ground there is around here, but they could've been made by anybody at any time."

"That's about the extent of what I saw," Ki agreed. "And with the ground hereabouts so rocky and hard, we might search all day without ever picking up any tracks to follow."

Jessie smiled a bit ruefully as she said, "Maybe we're being foolish trying to follow him, Ki. For all we know that might have been some lumberjack on his way into town or coming back from town and heading for his job."

"If it was, I must've startled him as much as he startled us. Let's go along to where we were headed, Jessie, the big redwood grove that Jerry Edmonds told us about."

"I was just getting ready to suggest that, Ki. And on the way back to town we can circle around to the timber stands and talk to some of the loggers. I have a pretty strong hunch we'll learn a lot more from them about what's really going on up here than we ever would if we just loafed around Mendocino City."

"Look, Ki!" Jessie exclaimed. She was reining in her horse as she gestured toward the vista ahead of them. "Even from a distance those trees are the most magnificent growing things I've ever seen. It's been such a long time since our last visit to the redwoods that I'd forgotten how huge and how beautiful they are."

"They have a good chance of staying that way for a long time, too, Jessie," Ki said as he pulled up his horse beside hers. "They're so far inland and the nearest river's such a long haul away that the timber operators will probably leave them alone."

"I suppose I could be called a timber operator," Jessie said thoughtfully, without taking her eyes off the redwood grove. "But even if there was the biggest river in the country close by, I don't believe I could ever think of those trees as something to be chopped down and sawed into boards."

For a few minutes both Jessie and Ki were silent, looking at the grove. The fifty or more redwood trees that formed it were indeed immense, their trunks so huge that no saw large enough to span them had yet been made. Their roots began arching out from the trunks high above the ground, more than twice the height of a tall man's head.

Far above the roots, along the massive trunks, branches twenty or thirty feet long thrust outward for a short distance below the place where the first older branches began. The bases of these higher branches had the bulk of small trees, and above them the lesser branches, with their dark green sprouting twigs, sloped to form long, vertical cones, constantly diminishing in size, to the tops of the magnificent trees.

"Let's ride on until we're in the middle of this grove," Jessie said to Ki. "I want to stop there for a while and dismount. I need to walk around a bit. I have a hunch that once we turn back toward the coast and get to the logging stands we're going to be too busy to come here for another visit."

Toeing their horses ahead, Jessie and Ki let their mounts set a leisurely pace as they rode into the grove.

Though there had been no noises outside it except for the gentle sighing of the light offshore breeze, the silence as they moved ahead seemed to become almost visible.

Neither Jessie nor Ki said anything as they moved slowly along. Now and then one of them would indicate something unusual about one of the giant trees, for each of the forest giants in the redwood stand seemed to have some special features that set it apart as an individual.

"Look, Ki!" Jessie exclaimed after they'd gotten deeper into the grove. She reined in, and as Ki stopped beside her she pointed toward one of the trees ahead. "There's just what I've been hoping we'd see."

Ki looked in the direction Jessie was pointing, then turned back and said, "If we're both looking at the same tree, you must see something about it that I'm missing."

"Don't you see, Ki?" Jessie asked. "That's the first of these trees we've seen with its main branches so close to the ground that I can reach one of them by standing up on my saddle!"

"Now, hold on, Jessie!" Ki cautioned as he pulled his horse to a halt beside hers. "Are you telling me that you're planning to try and climb one of these trees?"

"That's exactly what I intend to do!" she replied. "Ever since we got to this grove I've been looking for one with its main branches low enough for me to reach. This tree's the first one I've seen that I'm sure I can climb."

"Why do you want to climb one?" Ki asked. "I remember a few times when we were battling the cartel and had to climb a tree or a building wall or something like that, and you never seemed to enjoy it."

"That was different, Ki," Jessie said. "We were fighting for our lives then and we didn't have any choice. This is something I want to do because . . . well, because somehow I think it will make me feel that I'm part of the tree, part of this magnificent grove."

"And you don't think it's good enough just to look at them and enjoy them the way we've been doing?"

"It may be for some people, but I'd like to feel that I'm closer to the trees, Ki," she said. "I want to go as near to the top of this one as I can, and look out over the grove. I want to see the tops of the other trees without having to stand on the ground or sit here in my saddle and tilt my head back and strain to see those big branches up to their tallest tips."

Ki did not press the point or object any longer. He'd been Jessie's companion in many much more perilous situations than the one in which she was now proposing to place herself.

"Do you want me to climb with you?" he asked her. "I can loop my lariat around my shoulder and carry it along in case we get into a pinch where we need it to support us, either going up or climbing down."

Jessie shook her head as she replied, "No, Ki, but thanks for offering. I want to do this by myself."

"Well, it seems that you're set on doing it," Ki said. He was swinging out of his saddle as he spoke. "So I'll hold your horse while you stand up in your saddle and make your start up the tree. And I'll be ready to give you a hand if you get into any sort of trouble coming back to earth. It's always easier to climb up a tree than it is to climb down."

Jessie had already kicked her feet out of the stirrups and was twisting around to kneel on her mount's saddle. She levered herself to a standing position and reached up to grasp the highest stout limb that would support her weight, then swung free for a moment while groping

56

with her feet for the branch below the one to which she was clinging. A moment of twisting and turning passed while she sought and found a foothold on a lower branch; then she began ascending.

Ki looped the reins of their horses around a nearby sapling and moved back to the bole of the tree. He watched Jessie as she moved higher. The redwood tree's branches thrust out from its massive trunk at greater intervals as she climbed, and there were a few times when she had to hang free while swinging for a moment in midair until she could get a foot planted on a higher branch, but she persisted until she was within a few feet of the great tree's top.

"You should be up here with me, Ki," she called. "I can see for miles!"

"Thanks for the thought, Jessie, but I'll be satisfied just to stay here and help you get down," Ki replied.

"That'll be just as soon as I take one more good look around, Ki," Jessie told him. "You'd be surprised if you knew how far I can see. Why, I can look—"

Ki waited for a moment when Jessie stopped short. Then he asked, "What's wrong, Jessie? Something you see—"

"You wouldn't believe what I'm seeing, Ki!" she called. Her voice betrayed her surprise. "Just beyond the end of this stand of trees I'm looking at something neither of us believed in a little while ago! Ki, I'm looking at the Mendocino Monster himself!"

"This isn't any time for joking, Jessie," Ki told her. "If you've looked around enough to—"

"I'm not joking!" Jessie protested. "There's something I never expected to see between this stand of redwoods and the next one! Unless I'm very badly mistaken I am actually seeing the mysterious monster!"

"Oh, now, Jessie!" Ki said. "Your joke is—"

"I'm not joking, Ki!" Jessie's voice was sober as she went on, "Between this stand of redwoods and the next, there's some sort of hairy creature moving around. From here it looks huge. It's walking around like a man, but even if it does, I can tell that it's not a man. And I'm equally sure it's not a bear."

"You are serious, aren't you?" Ki was frowning as he spoke. "And you said it's moving around. Which way is it going?"

"It's—" Jessie stopped short and was silent for a moment, then she went on. "It's angling along toward the next redwood grove. Right now it's between this one and the other big grove off to our right."

"How far away is it?"

"I can't really be sure of the distance, Ki. This rolling country isn't like the prairie we're used to on the Circle Star. And looking down the way I am . . . well, I'd guess it's about two miles away. It's almost midway now, between the two redwood groves."

"Take a quick look around and pick up some landmarks that we can go by," Ki told her. "Then come on down. If your creature is that close—"

"It is!" Jessie broke in, her voice insistent.

Ki said, "Can we reach it before it gets into the trees?"

"I'm not sure, Ki. But we can certainly try!"

Jessie had been climbing down while she and Ki were talking. She halted, standing poised only a short distance above Ki, on one of the giant redwood's big lower branches.

"I'll have to swing down now," she said.

"I'm ready to catch you," Ki told her. "Come on down to the bottom branch, where I can stand under you, and

58

then let go of the branch whenever you're ready."

Jessie lowered herself to the bottom branch, and Ki moved along below it until he stood where he could catch her by taking a single step forward. She kneeled on the massive branch and looked down at him.

"I'm ready to drop now," she said. "Just let me know when you're directly below where I'll be landing."

Ki sidled along the ground, his head tilted back, his eyes fixed on Jessie, who was crouching now, peering at the ground.

"It's not a long drop now," he said. "And I'm ready to catch you."

Jessie twisted around on the massive bottom branch of the big redwood tree, then lay on her stomach to edge sidewise while still retaining her grasp on the branch. She twisted her torso around until only the grip of her hands on the deeply striated bark was supporting her.

"I'm ready if you are," she called without trying to make the awkward twist of her neck that would be required to keep her eyes on Ki.

"Let go, then," Ki called back.

Jessie released her grip and plummeted toward the ground. Ki stepped up as she was falling and caught her in his arms. The impact of her fall sent him toppling backward in spite of his braced legs, and they rolled for a while before they could get their arms and legs untangled. Then they stood for a moment, smiling at each other.

"We don't want to waste any time, Ki," Jessie said. "I've got a clear picture in my mind of the brush clump where I saw that thing—I guess that's the best way I can describe it. Let's mount up as fast as we can. I want to get to it before it can get away."

Chapter 6

Leaving the grove of majestic redwood trees, Jessie and Ki rode in a beeline to the brush clump where Jessie had spotted the moving figure between the two redwood groves.

"Are you sure you can find the place where you saw that thing?" Ki asked as their horses mounted the gently rising ground, heading for its crest.

"Of course I can," Jessie replied. "There's a little creek, or maybe it's a small river, that curves around beyond this slope. Whatever it was I saw—and I'm sure it must've been the thing folks up here call the Mendocino Monster—it was going down the slope toward the water."

Her voice was so positive that Ki did not ask her to elaborate on her description of the strange creature. They rode on in silence up the slope and reached its crest. Jessie reined in to look at the long stretch ahead and the sinuous line of thick brush that began at the bottom of the downslope.

"It's very odd, Ki," she said. "From here the ground doesn't look anything like it did when I was up in

61

that redwood tree. I don't know why, it just doesn't seem the same. But I'm sure about one thing—even if we haven't come in sight of it yet, the stream I saw that creature heading for is only a little way ahead of us."

"Quite likely it's still hidden by the underbrush," Ki suggested.

"I certainly hope so. I'm positive I wasn't just imagining what I saw there."

They forged ahead. When they finally broke through the stand of brush, there was no sign of water, but there was a maze of footprints on the soil of a riverbank. Ki could see more than enough of them to decide that Jessie could not have been mistaken. The prints were huge, blunt-ended ovals and were impressed deeply enough and spaced far enough apart to have been made by a giant who took long strides with long legs.

"Thank goodness!" Jessie breathed. "I was beginning to think I'd seen something that didn't exist!"

"Well, these footprints are certainly proof enough that you didn't, Jessie," Ki told her. "And I'm sure you're wondering about the same thing I am. They're not like most footprints we've tried to track in the past."

"So I noticed." She nodded. "They're just ovals, without any hint of which end is the toe and which is the heel. That means we're going to have to figure out which way that thing I saw was moving."

"We're bound to find a clue somewhere," Ki assured her.

"At least I can understand now why the folks around here are afraid of this mysterious creature." Jessie said, as she gazed at the big oval depressions. "From the size of those prints the feet that made them must be as big as a turkey platter."

"We can't be sure these prints were made by the monster, Jessie," Ki cautioned her. "And if whoever or whatever they were made by is of a size to match them, he'd have to be about as big as a small elephant."

"You don't think we're looking for a giant, do you?" Jessie frowned.

"If not a giant, then at least a big creature, I'd say, whether it's human or an animal. I'm ready to assume that these footprints were really made by the Mendocino Monster, but don't you think it's odd that nobody we've talked to has said anything about it being as big as these footprints and the spaces between them hint that he might be?"

"Perhaps that's because nobody seems to have gotten very close to him, except by accident. But let's try to follow the prints, Ki," Jessie suggested. "They look fairly fresh, and whoever made them, whether or not it was the creature, can't have gotten very far."

"We'd better lead the horses," Ki said. "Since we're going to be following foot tracks, walking will be just about as fast as going on horseback. Besides that, there'll be less chance of failing to see something on the ground that might give us a clue to whoever or whatever it is we're following."

"If we find that the footprints are leading us too far, we can always ride for a little while," Jessie said. "One good thing, Ki. These prints are certainly big enough to be seen whether we walk or ride."

Losing no more time, Jessie and Ki set out to follow the huge footprints. The impressions led them in a straight line for perhaps a quarter of a mile, then the soft sandy soil gave way abruptly to a long stretch of hard-surfaced broken earth. Now they found tracking the prints more difficult because of the ridges and humps of stone that had started to show as dark masses between thin patches of loose, windblown surface soil, which was often less than an inch deep on the underlying strata of stone.

For a short distance Jessie and Ki could no longer walk their horses side by side. They were forced to zigzag, for while the footprints still appeared from time to time, the surface of the ground had grown so rough and broken that it was difficult for them to be sure whether they were looking at a footprint or a hoofprint or at some natural indentation in the ground. Instead of walking easily with long steps, they moved at little better than a crawl.

After they'd been advancing for the better part of an hour, they saw another stand of redwoods ahead of them. A long, wide expanse of stumps at one side of the giant trees showed where loggers had been at work in the not too distant past. Jessie stopped where an uneven outcropping of stone rose above the sandy soil in a stretch of clear ground and divided the cut-over area from the redwood grove.

"As best I remember, Ki, this is about where I saw the creature," she said. "If we look around a little bit, we ought to find his footprints again."

Ki had been surveying the vista ahead while Jessie was talking. He shook his head as he replied, "This certainly isn't a place where it's going to be easy to track somebody, Jessie."

"I know." Jessie nodded. "The soil keeps changing, and here it's so thin and shifting and rocky that it won't hold footprints very long."

"If you've looked at the sky during these last few minutes, you've seen what I have," Ki went on. "Unless we hurry and cover as much ground as we can, there

64

won't be any tracks for us to find. Look at the clouds blowing toward us from the ocean. They're carrying rain in them, unless I'm very badly mistaken."

"Rain or no rain, I still think it's worth giving it a try, Ki. Perhaps if we separate and do some circling around we might be able to pick up some sort of trail."

"Yes, separating's a good idea," Ki agreed. "Suppose you keep to the high ground. I'll go down and follow the riverbank to see if I can find a place where it can be forded. If that rain catches us and it's a heavy one, we'll have to get to higher ground in a hurry."

"Our usual one-shot signal if, for some unforeseen reason, we're unable to see each other and one of us finds something interesting?" she asked.

"Of course. But we'll both be moving in more or less the same direction, so there's not much chance that we'll get too widely separated."

They parted then, and Ki zigzagged down to the edge of the stream. The river was neither wide nor deep, and its slow current ran glass-clear. Ki could see its sandy bottom, broken now and then by clusters of light-hued stones and all of it free of moss or other underwater growth. Dividing his attention between the stream and its banks, he walked in a zigzag pattern for a short distance, searching for signs that might indicate a regular crossing point.

He'd been moving along the erratic course of the streambed for only a short time when he glimpsed buildings ahead. They were on the opposite bank, and by their looks as Ki got closer he could identify them to his satisfaction as a small and long-deserted logging camp: bunkhouse, cookshack, and mess hall. From their dilapidated appearance, Ki judged that the buildings had been abandoned long ago.

Looking beyond the ramshackle structures he saw a sizeable spread of stumps, their tops moss-covered and the duff around them dark-hued, an indication that the camp had not been active for several years. He was standing at the edge of the river looking at the decaying buildings when he heard Jessie's call.

"Ki!" she shouted, "Ki! Call back to me so I can locate you! I've lost sight of you and I don't imagine you can see me any better than I can see you!"

"Here, Jessie!" Ki shouted.

He turned to go up the slope away from the river's edge, where Jessie could see him. When he reached the top of the slope and reoriented himself, he could see her in the distance. A moment later, as Ki was getting ready to call to her, Jessie saw him and waved, then started toward him. Ki settled back in his saddle to wait for her.

"I haven't seen any footprints for quite a while, Ki," she said as they got within speaking distance. "Have you?"

Ki shook his head as he replied, "No. Either the soil's changed and gotten too hard to hold footprints, or the monster has suddenly sprouted wings and flown away."

"Ki, both of us have done enough tracking to know that footprints don't just vanish of their own accord," Jessie frowned. "And since these have disappeared suddenly, it's safe to bet that if the creature really made them, he's wiped them out as he moved along, because he didn't want to leave a trail that could be followed."

A frown grew on Ki's face as he shook his head. He said, "No, Jessie. We don't know enough about it to assume he's smart enough to think of wiping out his footprints. Even if he did wipe them out, we'd have been sure to see a place that's been cleared, even on this hard, rocky ground. Are you sure this is where you saw the Mendocino Monster?"

"As sure as it's possible to be," she replied. "But we've had to go over so many of these stony, shifting stretches of ground since we started from the redwood grove that it's hard to be absolutely positive."

"I'll have to agree with you about that." Ki nodded. "All these bare places look alike. And, until now, whenever we lost the footprints we always managed to find them again by zigzagging. But by this time we've crisscrossed so much ground that it's hard to guess where we lost them."

"Maybe we didn't go far enough beyond the place where we saw the last set of footprints," Jessie suggested. "I'd like to push on before the rain begins, Ki. It's going to rain, there's no doubt about that, and if it's at all hard, there won't be any footprints left to find, much less to follow."

"That's possible, of course," Ki said thoughtfully. "Maybe we'd better go back to where we were, at the big bluff above the riverbed. I suppose he could've gone down to the river there, but the walls of the canyon it runs in were so steep and stony that it seems unlikely."

"He might have done that, Ki, but suppose he went in the direction opposite to the one we took."

"Downriver instead of upstream?"

"Yes." Jessie nodded. "If you remember, the wall of the canyon was sort of undercut there, and it looked like it'd be miserably hard going."

"Well, if it was really the monster you saw, he certainly didn't just vanish into thin air at the place where we turned to follow the prints," Ki frowned. "And I don't think—"

He stopped short when he saw Jessie's jaw drop in surprise as she gestured toward the river. Turning, Ki

saw that a woman had appeared suddenly on the opposite side of the stream. She was standing in front of
one of the dilapidated buildings of the long-abandoned
logging camp, staring at them, a puzzled frown forming
on her face.

Neither Jessie nor Ki spoke to her, and she said nothing, but stood examining them just as they were gazing
at her. The woman was neither old nor young, but her
features marked her as being either of Indian or Hispanic
origin. She wore a simple dress that fell in a straight line
from her shoulders to her knees. Its fabric still retained
the hint of a print design, but it was so faded that at first
glance it seemed colorless.

Jessie waited for a moment, then decided to take
the initiative. Waving at the woman she called, "Hello,
there! If this is where you live, maybe you can help us."

For a moment the woman did not reply. Then she
asked, "Who you are? From where you come? What
you do here?"

"We've come here from Mendocino City, where we're
visiting," Jessie replied. "But we live in Texas. My
companion's name is Ki, and mine is Starbuck, Jessica
Starbuck. I'm sure you must know about the Starbuck
Mill that I own in Mendocino."

Ignoring Jessie's remarks as though she had not heard
them, the woman asked, "You look for somebody? Is
only me here."

Now it was Jessie's turn to act as though she'd suddenly become deaf. Instead of answering she asked, "Do
you stay here all the time by yourself?"

"Me, myself, yes," the woman replied.

"Doesn't anybody else ever come here?" Jessie
pressed.

Her eyes widening, the woman replied, "No."

"And you don't get lonesome?" Ki asked.

Before she could reply to Ki's question, a rumble of thunder announced the arrival of the rain. Before the sound had faded, big drops began falling, spattering on the hard ground. A short distance away the heart of the suddenly oncoming rainstorm obscured the landscape in a shimmering curtain of silver.

Ignoring Ki's question now, the woman indicated a spot a few yards upstream, where sparkles of spattering water gleamed now and then. "Cross there," she said. Then she gestured toward the nearest of the ramshackle structures and said, "Come. We will be dry inside."

Jessie and Ki hurried to cross the stream and followed the woman when she led them to the nearest and largest of the dilapidated buildings. As she stepped up onto its narrow porch and disappeared through the door, they dismounted and quickly tethered their horses to one of the posts that supported the sagging roof. Then they followed the woman into the building.

She had stopped just inside the door. Jessie and Ki halted beside her and looked around. The room they'd entered was large, taking in half of the structure, and its lack of furniture made it seem even more cavernous. The big room was dim, almost dark, but Jessie and Ki could see three doorways in its rear wall. A heavy coat of grime covered the small pairs of windows set into each of its side walls, and the faint light that came through the door by which they'd entered did little to add to its brightness.

"You stay till rain stops," the woman said. She gestured toward the doorways in the back wall and went on, "Rooms there. Sleep."

Before Jessie or Ki could ask any questions the woman disappeared through the center door in the room's rear wall. For a moment Jessie and Ki exchanged questioning looks. At last Jessie broke the silence.

"I'd say we've had a rather strange welcome, Ki," she said. "But perhaps it's not wise to bother that woman with a lot of questions. We'll have time for that later. It's going to be dark early; I'd say within the next half hour or so. We're certainly better off being inside rather than out in that driving rain."

"I don't know what to make of it, either," Ki replied. "And speaking of rain, I'd better get our gear in here before it gets soaked. From the look of those clouds, we're likely to want to stay here awhile."

When Ki left, Jessie began walking around the big room that spanned the front of the building. It was bare except for a cookstove in which no fire burned, a scarred and battered table, and three or four chairs. She glanced into the rooms indicated by the woman. They were sparsely furnished, a bed and chair in each small chamber. By the time Jessie had finished her inspection, Ki returned, carrying their dripping saddlebags.

"You're right about us being here for a while, Jessie," he said. "I dropped our saddles on the porch, and I'm sure the rain won't bother the horses. But there's no sign of any break in those rain clouds."

"At least we won't be soaked, Ki. And I looked into those rooms. There's a bed in each of them. I think we'd better use them; at least we'll be spared sleeping on the floor or in the rain. And riding back to town in this kind of weather is something I'd just as soon avoid."

"Then we'll make the best of things." Ki shrugged.

"Which we've had to do before," Jessie went on. "I can't think of anything to do except eat a bite before it gets too dark to see what we're eating. Then we'll just turn in and sleep while we're waiting for the rain to stop."

They had a quick meal, eating in virtual silence. The darkness deepened as they ate, and their eyes adjusted to night vision as the faint light faded. When they'd finished their spartan supper and pushed away from the table, Jessie said, "It'll be dark in a few minutes, Ki, and there isn't anything I can think of to keep us from turning in. That's what I intend to do without waiting any longer."

"And I won't be sorry to follow your example, Jessie. Do you have any preference between the rooms?"

"As far as I could tell when I glanced into them, they're almost exactly alike. And I'm sure that our hostess doesn't care any more than we do. But my gear's closer to the room on the right, so I'll just take the line of least resistance and sleep in it."

Ki nodded and started for the left-hand door. The single high, grime-crusted window in the small room allowed a little of the lighter gloom outside to trickle through its pane, and Ki had no trouble stepping through the semidarkness to the bed. He did not bother to undress, but stretched out immediately on the lumpy mattress. Within a few minutes he was sleeping soundly.

Though the noise was almost inaudible, the metallic tick of the closing door was loud enough in the stillness to awaken Ki. He sat up in bed, one hand reaching to the pillow beside him, groping for the leather case that contained his *shuriken*. He was sliding one of the throwing blades from the case when the voice of the woman who'd greeted him and Jessie broke the stillness.

"Do not worry," she said. "I have not come to harm you. I was sleeping, and when I waked up my first thought was of you being here. Then I thought of the woman with you. I am glad you are not with her, for I have been too long without a man."

For a moment Ki was too astonished to reply. His eyes had adjusted to the darkness now, and he could see the woman. She'd reached the bed and was standing beside it, visible only as a ghostly outline against the faint tinge of skylight that trickled through the room's lone window. He watched silently as she shrugged and her silhouette seemed to ripple as her dress slipped from her shoulders to the floor, and even in the darkness Ki could see that she now stood naked.

At last Ki found his voice. He said, "Our needs are the same. You're very welcome."

★
Chapter 7

Without speaking, the woman lay down beside Ki. Even as he was turning toward her, she had placed her hand on his ribs and was sliding it down his body. When it reached his crotch, she stopped its downward movement; then her fingers spread to cradle him. Ki remained motionless for the first few moments of her caresses. After his erection began, he responded to her attentions by bringing his own hands into play. His fingers moved as swiftly and surely as hers had, but Ki's moves were guided by the experiences and teachings he'd had in his visits to geisha houses and other encounters he'd had with women while growing to maturity in the Orient.

For the first moments after his fingertips touched his uninvited companion's unexpectedly soft skin Ki moved them as lightly as so many feathers. He sent them dancing across her full breasts until their tips grew firm, protruding from the dark pink, pebbled aureoles that surrounded them. Now Ki bent to replace his fingers with his lips and tongue. Almost at once her body started to twitch.

Loving the occasional shudders that rippled through her body, she was soon matching Ki's caresses, but her attentions were confined to his crotch. Her hands seemed to move of their own volition until several minutes had passed and the mild twitchings of her torso had grown more pronounced. The clumsy random movements of her hands ended, and her fingers closed around him and grasped him firmly. When she realized that he had swollen to the utmost, she released him and fell back on the mattress, her thighs sprawled open.

Ki did not accept her tacit invitation at once. He lay motionless for a moment before realizing that he was in bed with a woman who was not accustomed to the subtleties of Oriental sexual foreplay. He did not continue trying to arouse her, but moved to crouch above her and let her place him, then drove instantly with a lusty thrust to make a full penetration.

Her response was immediate and vigorous. She locked her ankles around Ki's hips while he continued his deep, deliberate lunges. Much sooner than Ki had expected her torso squirmed and her hips began to rock in a sort of twisting spiral. Ki began to drive with increased vigor, and the woman squirming beneath him matched his thrusts by gyrating her hips in a constantly accelerating rhythm.

Now Ki began to call into play the sexual skills he'd learned from the geishas, in the scores of pleasure houses he'd visited during his youthful years of aimless wandering. When he felt his partner's body begin to quiver, he did not drive at all, but pressed himself to her firmly, pinning her motionless until he felt her beginning throes fade and come to an end.

Always at such moments Ki rested with her for a short while, still buried fully and without allowing his erection to diminish. Each time when he resumed stroking, she responded with fresh enthusiasm, and now her need for immediate fulfillment seemed to wane.

Ki repeated this action three times, until she could no longer control her urge to fulfillment. Her initial waves of small shivers now led her to a writhing, gasping, explosive spasm. She loosed small cries of pleasure as her body continued to quiver; then her cries trailed away and died as she fell back, inert. She lay almost totally still for a short while, then moved as though to leave him. Ki embraced her and held her motionless before he started stroking once more.

Once again the woman peaked quickly and her form was again seized by throbbing shudders. This time Ki did not exercise his control, but joined her in terminal gratification. He did not try to keep her with him after they'd stopped, but rolled away and stretched out. To his surprise the woman lay inert for a few moments after her climax had passed; then, still without having spoken, she sat up and left the bed. Ki watched her shadowy form until she disappeared through the door.

During the entire span of their encounter neither of them had spoken. As the door closed behind her, Ki stretched out with a contented sigh. Then he shifted to his favored sleeping position, on his back, and relaxed until deep slumber claimed him.

"After last night's rain, we might have a better chance of picking up the monster's trail," Jessie suggested.

She and Ki were sitting in the main room of the dilapidated bunkhouse, making a pickup breakfast from what edibles were left of their saddle rations. They'd looked through the place for the woman who'd greeted

75

them the previous evening, but she'd disappeared without a trace. Puzzled but not alarmed by her absence, they had decided to eat their breakfast and do a bit more exploring as they returned to town.

"I'll agree that the possibilities are better than yesterday's," Ki told Jessie as they discussed their plans. "We're going to have a problem trying to find a place to start, though. I'm guessing, but it's very likely that the rain last night washed away any prints he might've made after we got our last glimpse of him."

"But that's to our advantage, Ki," Jessie said. "You're quite right about all of the old footprints hereabouts being destroyed by the rain, but if he's moving around at all today we'll have fresh prints to follow."

"You intend to keep looking for him, then?"

"I'm not quite sure whether I want to keep on looking now, or put it off until we've finished with our business at the mill, Ki." She frowned.

"What about the mill, Jessie?" he asked. "After all, that's what brought us up here."

"Oh, the mill will still be there when we get back to town. So will Jerry Edmonds, and I'm sure he's wondering where we've gotten off to. And I'm almost equally sure that the unpleasant Mr. Harper will be looking for us as well, probably with some new offer to buy me out."

"Of course you'll tell him again that you're not interested in his offer," Ki smiled.

"Certainly. And perhaps this time he'll believe me. But I suppose we had better go back to town, Ki. By this time the mill hands will have heard that you and I are here in Mendocino, and there'll be all sorts of rumors flying around."

"And the quicker they're settled, the better off all of us will be," Ki observed.

"Settling them won't take long. And as curious as I've gotten about the Mendocino Monster, we'd better put off trying to find out about him until I'm sure that I've worked out all the difficulties with the mill. That's really what brought us here."

"Then I'd say it's time for us to mount up and go," Ki told her. "I'll get the horses ready, and we can be on our way."

"I've been worried about you and Ki," Jerry Edmonds told Jessie as he reached the hitch rail in front of the Starbuck Mill's main building. Jessie and Ki had just dismounted and were tethering their horses. "I was expecting you to move out here from the hotel yesterday. When you didn't show up, I began wondering where you were."

"It was thoughtless of me not to send word that Ki and I decided take a ride to the nearest redwood grove," Jessie said.

"So the desk clerk told me." Edmonds nodded. "I was really concerned last night when that rain started. I stopped at the hotel again on my way home, but they said you and Ki had left and still hadn't gotten back."

"Then you must've gotten some of the rainstorm here in town," Jessie said. She paused for a moment, trying to decide whether to mention their distant glimpse of the monster. She decided quickly to omit it and went on. "But the answer to where Ki and I were is very simple. We decided to take a longer ride inland than we'd planned because I wanted to look at some of the older redwood groves."

"You didn't have to travel very far to find them, Jessie." Edmonds frowned. "Did the rain bother you, that far inland?"

"Oh, it caught us, all right," Jessie assured him. "But luckily we'd stumbled onto an old abandoned logging camp before the real downpour started, so we stayed there last night."

"I don't suppose you even thought about the possibility that it might've been one of yours," Edmonds went on. "There are several of those deserted camps hereabouts, including a few that're Starbuck property."

"It didn't occur to me to ask, and I don't suppose Ki gave it a thought." Jessie smiled.

"I'll admit that I didn't think of it either," Ki put in.

"Neither of us could think about much except getting out of the rain," Jessie went on. "We could see the rainstorm coming at us and were just glad to find some shelter."

"You're lucky you didn't get soaked," Edmonds observed. "Even the lumberjacks who're used to this Mendocino climate sometimes get pneumonia after they've been caught in one of those cold rainstorms."

"A good soaking in warm water is what I feel I need right now." Jessie smiled. "And I know how limited the bathing accomodations are, out here at the mill. So Ki and I will move into our new quarters a little bit later, after we've gone back to the hotel to get our luggage."

"There are plenty of spare hands here," Edmonds suggested. "Why don't I just send one or two of them to pick up whatever you've left at the hotel?"

"Thank you, Jerry," Jessie replied. "But Ki and I haven't yet started packing to move out here. Besides, I prefer to have us do our own packing. And I've also got to settle the hotel bill. It's not a big item, but I don't want to bother your office help with handling our personal expenses."

"Well, that's easy to understand." Edmonds nodded. "I'll be knocking at your door when you come back, then. And whenever you're ready, we can sit down together and talk about the mill's problems." He paused momentarily before adding, "Which I'm sorry to say are mostly my problems, of course."

"Yes, I'm afraid you're right," she agreed. "Most of them are. But we've had a few rough places to smooth out before. I'm sure we can work out the new ones, too."

With a final glance around the tousled hotel room, Jessie said, "If you're through gathering up your things from your room, Ki, you might as well take our saddlebags down to the horses. I'll pick up these few loose things and bundle them under my arm. If you'll give me your room key, I'll stop at the desk and settle our account on my way to join you."

Ki nodded and handed Jessie his key. Then he picked up their saddlebags and left. Passing through the lobby with a nod at the idle desk clerk, he reached the street and draped the saddlebags over the backs of their tethered horses, then stepped back to the door to wait for Jessie. Though the street on which the hotel stood was one of the town's usually busy thoroughfares, it was almost totally deserted at that hour of the early afternoon. Only an occasional hurrying pedestrian was visible, and none of them were close to the hotel door.

After he'd waited for what seemed an exceptionally long time, Ki stepped inside the door. Through the narrow arch at the end of the short hall he could get a glimpse of only a part of the reception desk, and he took the few steps necessary to enable him to see the entire lobby and the wide arch that opened into the dining room.

Jessie was nowhere in sight. The only occupant of the narrow lobby was the desk clerk, who was busy checking the small tier of pigeonholes behind the registration desk. Taking a long stride into the lobby, Ki glanced through the open double doors leading into the dining room, but none of the tables were occupied. No afternoon drinkers stood at the bar, and the barkeeper was not in his usual place behind the polished mahogany.

Ki's normally inscrutable face formed a frown. He went to the desk, but the clerk had disappeared. Ki tapped the call bell. When the desk clerk came in through the door at one end of the long, highly polished check-in desk, Ki asked, "Have you seen Miss Starbuck? I've been waiting for her outside. She intended to stop here and settle our account. But I've been waiting quite some time and she still hasn't shown up."

"Well, I didn't see her come through here," the desk clerk replied. "And I ain't been away none till just a minute ago. I seen the check-in register needed some new pages and went back to the closet to get some. If she'd stopped before I got back here to the desk, she'd've likely hit the call bell, but I ain't heard it, so I don't guess she rung it."

"I'm sure she wouldn't have gone out the back door." Ki frowned. "It would make no sense, because she knew our horses are at the front hitch rail. If she had come out the front door, I'd have seen her. More than likely she's still in her room. It just might be taking her longer than she'd expected to do her packing. I'll go take a look."

Ki went down the long carpeted corridor and turned at the hallway that led to the rooms he and Jessie had occupied. The door to Jessie's room was ajar, though Ki was positive that he'd closed it when he carried

80

their saddlebags out to the horses. He pushed through and stepped into the room.

Jessie was nowhere in sight, but her half-packed suitcase was still lying where he'd noticed it earlier, spread open on the bed. A small heap of her clothing lay beside the suitcase, and Ki took its presence as proof that she had not finished packing.

Thinking that Jessie might have gone into his deserted room for a final look around, Ki took another few steps down the corridor to give the room a second inspection. Its appearance had not changed since he'd left it, and Jessie was not inside. Now a worried frown started to pucker Ki's usually placid face. He returned to the hall and looked along it in both directions.

He could see that there was no one except the clerk at the registration desk. In the opposite direction there were two more room doors on each side of the hall as well as a door at the end of the passage. All of them were closed. Ki tried the room doors in turn, and when he discovered that both of them were locked, he pressed an ear to each one, but heard no sounds.

Now the worried frown that had flickered across Ki's face became a fixture. He stood motionless for a moment before returning to the registration desk.

"Are you absolutely sure that you haven't gotten a glimpse of Miss Starbuck since I went outside?" he asked the clerk.

"Well, now, if I'd seen her, I'd've told you I did when you asked me about her a minute ago," the man replied.

"And there hasn't been anyone going past the desk here since I left?" Ki frowned as he asked the question.

"Nary a soul," the clerk assured him, then added, "Nobody but you."

"What about those rooms past Miss Starbuck's and mine, the ones between them and the end of the hall?" Ki pressed. "Who's occupying them?"

"Nobody is, right now. The boss is having new wallpaper put up in 'em. We ain't been renting 'em since the paperhangers begun working, about a week ago."

"Then I don't suppose you'd have any objections to letting me look in them?" Ki asked.

"What for?" The clerk frowned. "I wasn't lying to you when I told you them rooms is empty."

"It's not that I doubt what you told me, but I have the unfortunate need to see them myself," Ki replied.

After a moment of thoughtful silence the clerk shrugged and said, "I can't see why you're so all-fired het up to look at them rooms, but if it'll make you feel any better I don't reckon it'll hurt none for you to see 'em. Come along. I'll just step along down the hall with you and open 'em to let you look in."

Reaching below the desktop, the clerk produced a large key ring that held a single key. He rounded the end of the check-in counter and started down the hall with Ki beside him.

As they passed the half-open door of Jessie's room, the clerk glanced inside and shrugged, then moved on to the doors at the opposite end of the corridor. He unlocked each of them in turn, and Ki stepped in to examine them. Neither of the two held anything except ladders, rolls of wallpaper, paste buckets, and an array of miscellaneous tools on the floor.

"You satisfied now?" the clerk asked when Ki returned to join him.

"Yes, I have learned what I needed to know." Ki nodded. "And you're sure that Miss Starbuck didn't go past you while you were at the front desk?"

"Just like I told you, I didn't see her nor nobody else pass by. Excepting you, of course."

"Then she must have gone out the back door." Ki frowned. "And that'd be a very odd thing for her to do, because I was waiting with her horse and mine at the front of the building."

"Well, you know how women can be sometimes," the clerk said, more than a tinge of commiseration in his voice. "You think you're getting along with 'em just fine, but all of a sudden they get choosey and walk away from a fellow."

Ki did not take the time that he was sure would be needed to explain his relationship with Jessie. Even before the clerk had finished his observations on the futility of trusting women, Ki was digging a gold double eagle out of his pouch. He dropped the coin on the counter, where it danced for a second or two of small tinklings.

"Put this against the account you have for Miss Starbuck and me," he said. "Use whatever's needed to pay one of your stable hands to tend to the extra horse I'll be leaving outside. When Miss Starbuck and I get back, we'll settle accounts with both you and the hotel."

Before the astonished clerk had assimilated the crisp instructions, Ki had turned and was heading for the door. He was pushing it open when the man at the desk called to him.

"Hey, there! If you're checking out, you got to settle up proper! Come on back here, now—"

Ki neither stopped nor replied. He pushed through the door, gathered up the reins of his horse, and was swinging into the saddle when the desk clerk burst from the door. He was waving a paper with an upraised hand; Ki took it to be the hotel bill.

Over his shoulder he called, "Don't worry about your bill! I've told you what to do, and you'll be well paid if you carry out my instructions! Right now I've got more important business to attend to!"

Reining his horse around, Ki headed for the alley behind the hotel building. Dismounting at the back door of the big structure, he let his mount stand while he examined each inch of the alley around the doorway. The narrow little passageway was unpaved, the packed dirt of its surface dotted here and there with small glistening puddles remaining from the previous day's rain showers, which formed a crisscrossed maze in which hoofprints and bootprints overlapped.

To Ki the rounded palm-sized puddles meant the hoofprints of horses, and he began examining them closely. Only a tracker as expert as he was could have made sense of the prints in the clutter that dotted the ground, but Ki had been taught the art of reading sign by Alexander Starbuck's Indian friends. He'd learned still more during the years when he and Jessie were battling side by side to avenge her father's murder.

Though he was sure several times that he'd spotted the small prints of Jessie's boots, it was not until he'd worked his way a short distance from the door that he was positive he'd discovered what he'd been seeking.

Ki's inch-by-inch study of the ground had led him away from the door in a series of circlings and half-circlings to a point where the most confused maze of prints diminished. On the less cluttered earth he saw a partial print that he was positive had been left by one of Jessie's small boots. The little depression had almost been obliterated by the semicircle of a horse's hoofprint.

From the maze of confused and overlapping prints at the alley's end, Ki realized that there was only one answer to Jessie's disappearance. At the point where he was now standing, Jessie had mounted a horse, and with other riders flanking her on each side, she had ridden— or had been forced to ride—away from the alley behind the hotel.

★
Chapter 8

Once again Jessie tested the thongs that lashed her wrists to her mount's saddle horn. The tough leather strips had no more slack now than they had when she'd first tried them. Her persistent, futile efforts only repeated those she'd begun soon after the men who'd captured her started on the trail.

Thinking back, Jessie tried to recall how many hours had passed since she'd been tied to her saddle by the two men who had appeared in her hotel room almost as silently as though they'd materialized from thin air. She glanced at the sky, but the layers of clouds that had drifted in from the ocean now hid the sun. Jessie realized that the hour might as easily be morning or midday or afternoon.

Although at the time when the intruders grabbed her, Jessie's holstered Colt and gunbelt had been lying on the bed beside her saddlebags, ready to be put on, she could not reach them before the two men seized her and held her motionless. Jessie had been standing beside the bed, bending over it to tighten the saddlebag's straps when she heard the whisper of feet on the carpeted floor. Her certainty that the almost inaudible footsteps indicated that Ki was returning to help with her luggage had been so great that she did not look around.

Jessie's first hint of danger was the hamlike hand that swept over her shoulder and clamped across her mouth to insure her silence while a muscular arm encircled her torso. The onslaught had been so totally unexpected that her quick reaction had been useless.

At the same time the first man closed his hand over her mouth, the other plug-ugly was passing a looped rope around her upper body to hold her arms motionless. The moment he was sure that his loop was tight, he secured her wrists behind her back with a short rope noose, brought the end of the loop up around her chest, and took a turn around her throat.

With the looped rope binding her arms to hold her helpless and the noose circling her throat and threatening to choke her with each move she made, Jessie had not been able to fight back. The men who'd invaded her room had done their work so quickly that she'd had no chance to bring into play the *tai quon do* attacks that she'd learned from Ki. Moving with the skill of professional thugs, the men had completed their surprise capture with a quick and silent job of binding a bandana kerchief across Jessie's lips.

Holding Jessie between them by the ropes that criss-crossed her upper body, they forced her to walk with them down the short length of the deserted corridor between her room and the doorway at the end of the hall. Jessie needed only to glance at the three waiting horses to know what they planned to do.

Trying to leave a clue that Ki might find, she stomped her booted feet as hard as she dared while they crossed the alley to the horses. The grinding of gravel under her boot soles did nothing but discourage her, for she could scarcely hear the noise.

After they'd lifted her into the saddle of one of the three waiting horses, they made quick work of adjusting her bonds. Holding her feet securely in the stirrups, they'd lashed them in place with strips of leather, then bound her wrists to the saddle horn. Within two or three minutes after leaving the hotel, the men had mounted their own horses and were leading her out of the alley.

Jessie's hopes for a rescue had soared momentarily when they reached the street, but it bore no traffic in either direction. With Ki waiting for her in front of the hotel, Jessie realized at once that her bonds and the gag in her mouth would prevent her from making the sort of disturbance that might have attracted his attention.

All that she could do was to sit motionless in the saddle as the two men who'd captured her toed their horses to a faster walk, quickly crossed the thorough-fare, and reined their mounts onto the vestigial trail that led away from town. They were soon beyond the half-dozen houses that were scattered on a small strip of land between the street and the rugged country ahead.

For the first few moments after they'd started, when Jessie's captors were leading her mount along the faint trail, she'd glanced hopefully at the little dwellings, but had seen no signs of life behind their shuttered windows and closed doors.

Though Jessie was far from giving up, she realized the futility of trying to free herself at the moment. She relaxed as much as possible and devoted her attention to studying her surroundings while the men holding her prisoner led her to some destination still unknown.

As Ki set out to follow the trail he hoped would lead him to wherever Jessie's captors had led her, his feeling of frustration began to form even before he'd reached the point, a bare half-mile from town, where the night's rainfall had ended. The showers had been light compared to the winter rains. Only in the few areas where there were no heavy stands of trees had the rain softened the soil enough for it to take and hold the hoofprints left by the horses which Jessie and her abductors had been riding.

He encountered many long stretches of road where no rain had fallen. In such places the surface of the half-road, half-trail he was following had held only the hints of hoofprints. Along some of them Ki was unable to tell with any certainty whether he was still following the same hoofprints he'd picked up at the edge of town.

By the time he'd reached this point, however, he was carrying in his mind a strong picture of the hoofprint patterns, and he could hold his own, even where the earth was still hard and thickly studded with rocks.

After moving forward at a snail's pace for a short distance, Ki found that despite his skill as a tracker he was often forced to stop and dismount while he zigzagged on foot, seeking a stretch of earth where he could get a clear look at the few footprints and hoofprints that were barely visible on the hard-packed soil of the inland trail.

He kept reminding himself that these vestiges of tracks were too sparse to be considered foolproof guides. Then he quickly rebutted his own conclusions when he realized that they were quite likely the only signs he was going to encounter as he continued to trail Jessie and her captors. Always in Ki's mind there was the thought of Jessie being in the hands of a gang whose members would have no scruples in their treatment of her.

Nor did Ki doubt for a moment that he knew the identity of the person who was responsible for Jessie's abduction. Only one man fitted the pattern of events, and that man was Vance Harper. Recalling the brief interchange between Jessie and Harper on the evening he and Jessie had arrived in Mendocino, Ki could think of no one else who had more reason to stage her kidnapping.

Harper had announced openly in his first conversation with Jessie that he intended to become the kingpin lumber supplier on the Mendocino coast. He'd also hinted that he cared little whether he gained his goal by purchase or by intimidation. Ki was positive that when he'd caught up with Jessie's kidnappers he would find that somehow Harper had engineered her abduction, maybe by paying the thugs to capture Jessie and carry her to some isolated spot, which it had now become Ki's own challenge to discover.

Ki was ready to follow their trail wherever it might lead him, for his first concern was to find Jessie and free her as quickly as possible. While the thoughts of her predicament that flashed through his mind were anything but pleasant, they did not interfere with his painstaking examination of the small, faint, and often frustrating trail signs that were all he had to go by.

Among the few items Ki noted with a feeling of satisfaction was that one of the two men who he was sure had captured Jessie could be counted on to ease his tracking job. The horse that the man rode lacked a calk on the arch at the top of its left hind shoe, which provided a positive and unmistakable sign to follow.

Even at the slow pace he was forced to move, Ki could not disregard the feeling of progress that grew stronger as his painstaking search bore fruit. He had become convinced that he was holding an ace in the hole, and his rising spirits led him to abandon his slow inch-by-inch search of the trail. He'd succeeded in following the trio of riders until he came to a point where the road forked. One of the branches continued in a more or less straight line toward the redwood stands; the other led north.

Reining in, Ki studied the soft, almost liquid surface of the offshoot trail. Looking at the downsloping terrain ahead, he could see that the fork leading north deteriorated rapidly into a soft muddy morass. The landscape on all sides was a series of shining puddles of water.

Although Ki was not certain that he wasn't missing something because the puddled ground would not retain hoofprints for more than a few minutes, he returned his attention to the more clearly marked path. There were more prints than he'd expected to see dotting its surface, but after he'd ridden along it for a short distance, Ki could once again distinguish the fresh pocks from the older hoofprints in the dark soil.

Relaxing a bit following his discovery, Ki toed his horse onto the firmer ground beside the trail and continued his slow pace. The trail passed through one patch of stumps after another, and now its direction could not be misjudged.

Ki saw that it was taking him toward the tips of the tall pines, which rose above a few occasional clumps of small beginning redwood growth. He could see that the ground began to level off beyond the trees, but the sagging lower branches of the pines hid much of this area. Ki pulled up his horse and spent the next few moments trying to select the best spot at which to enter the grove.

● ● ●

Jessie had learned nothing as yet about the motives of the two men who'd captured her. Their conversation had been scanty and carried on in low voices; she'd been able to hear only a few words, and all that she'd discovered was their names. The taller of the two was Lem; the other was Brace.

The only other things she heard were remarks about saloons and women, until she attracted their attention with her stifled efforts to talk. She looked from one to the other, bending her head from side to side and trying to send signals with her eyes. At last the one who appeared to be the leader responded by removing her gag.

As soon as her lips were free and she had taken a few deep breaths, Jessie said, "If we have much further to go and you expect me to be alive when we get to wherever it is you're taking me, I'll certainly need to be able to breathe. That gag has been choking me, and if you're worried about me calling out or shouting, I'm ready to promise that I won't, as long as I can breathe freely."

Neither of the outlaws spoke for a moment while they exchanged questioning glances; then the man who seemed to be in charge of her abduction said, "You figure we're going to believe you? Why, you'd likely yell your head off if we was to leave off that gag."

"From what I've seen so far, I doubt very strongly that there's anybody on this trail to hear me. The very least you can do is to leave that gag loose enough for me to breathe," she insisted. "What will the man who's hiring you say if all you bring him is my dead body?"

"What she says makes sense, Brace," the second abductor agreed. "And there sure ain't nobody around here that'd hear her even if she did yell."

"I reckon you're right," Brace replied. "But be smart, Lem. Just loosen her gag enough so that she can breathe easy."

While the slightly relaxed pressure of the gag eased Jessie's discomfort, she realized that she still knew nothing about the two men except that they had names, which she could remember against a future time. She resigned herself to being silent, at least for the moment, while they continued to lead her horse inland at a steady pace. The terrain over which they moved bore a resemblance to the small portion of the Mendocino coast that she and Ki had seen on their previous day's excursion, though she had not seen any groves of majestic redwoods. On two or three occasions Jessie had sighted a stream in the distance, but she'd been unable to tell whether she was looking at a small river or a large creek; nor could she determine whether she'd seen only one stream flowing in a sinuous course or a large stream and some of its small feeders.

Only once had there been any evidence of logging. In what Jessie thought of as a long expanse, the land on both sides of the narrow road had been dotted with closely spaced stumps and covered with browning branches. She needed no one to tell her that she was looking at evidence that at some fairly recent time loggers had cleared the land and moved on. It provided a striking contrast to the young forest that had become visible now in the constantly shifting haze ahead of them.

"Where you figure on going when we get paid off for this job?" Lem asked after they had ridden in silence for perhaps another quarter of an hour.

"I don't figure to go noplace," Brace replied. "Mendocino's plenty good enough for me. As long as Harper keeps his mouth shut, we ain't got a thing to worry about."

"Maybe so, Brace. But maybe not. Don't forget, he told us that he wanted us to make ourselves scarce after we brought him the woman."

A grunt that could have meant anything was the first reply given by Brace. Then after a moment of silence he said, "I reckon you know why." When Lem replied by shaking his head, Brace went on, "I got a real strong hunch that Harper's figuring to get rid of the woman."

"Well, that ain't our business, is it?" Lem asked. Then he went on, "All we was ever supposed to do is hand her over to him. Then we get our pay, and do what he said for us to do, make ourselves scarce. Whatever Harper does after that's not any of our business."

"Don't be a damn fool!" Brace snapped. "You think a bastard mean as Harper's going to leave us two hanging around? Why, right now we know more'n just a little bit about what he's up to. By the time we wind up this job he's got us doing we'll have enough on him to keep him awake at night every time he thinks about us."

"Why, he oughta know there ain't no cause for him to worry about you and me," Lem replied. "If there were, he wouldn't've give us this kind of job."

"I thought about that some myself, Lem," Brace said. "But you got to agree, this ain't the same kinda thing we been doing for Harper. Suppose he does take a notion to get rid of this dame?"

"Then he'd get the blame for it, not us."

Brace snorted derisively, then said, "When you got outa bed this morning you must've left your brains on the pillow. Ain't you got sense enough to know that when Harper pays us for grabbing this dame and then takes her off someplace and gets rid of her, the law says we're as guilty as he is?"

Now Jessie spoke for the first time since her gag had been loosened. She said, "You're right about that, of course. The law calls it an accessory to murder, and if Vance Harper should be foolish enough to kill me, all three of you would go to the gallows."

Brace and Lem exchanged frowning glances; then Brace said, "Put that gag back on her! We don't have to listen to anything she'd say!"

"Please! Wait a minute!" Jessie said before Lem could reach for her gag. "I'll be quiet. All three of us know that I haven't a chance in the world to get away from you. I'm not interested in saying anything to the sheriff or constable or whoever has the job of enforcing the law here. The only person I want to talk to is the man who's hiring you."

"Well, it won't be very long before you can do that," Brace assured her. "Give or take another half hour, we'll be to where we're taking you. Soon as we hand you over to the man that's waiting for us, our job's finished. Then me and Lem aim to cut a shuck fast as we can for someplace where the law ain't going to bother us."

"From what I heard you say earlier, the man who's expecting you to hand me over to him is Vance Harper," Jessie went on. "He'd certainly have been able to manage getting you into the hotel, and he'd also have found out which room I was occupying, as well as arranging a few other minor things such as being sure none of the hotel employees would be around to interfere. Am I right?"

"Now, I ain't going to say yes and I ain't going to say no to that," Brace replied.

"That's right!" Lem agreed. "Just let her go on guessing."

"I take that to mean I'm right in my assumptions, then," Jessie said.

There was no triumph in her voice, just a firm assertion that she had not been mistaken. Jessie fell silent then, scanning the landscape to memorize its features. She was certain that by this time Ki was well along in making a search for her, and she was equally certain that he'd find her.

★
Chapter 9

Jessie had been true to her promise. She had not said a word while they were moving; nor did she speak when the men who'd captured her stopped to rest the horses after topping the big ridge. The day was already well along, and she'd half-expected them to dismount for a leg stretch, but they did not. They merely shifted in their saddles for a few minutes while picking up their earlier conversation at the point where it had stopped.

More than once they speculated about the most advantageous moves they might make after they'd delivered Jessie to Vance Harper. She recognized the names of some of the outlaw leaders that they mentioned and was surprised that they made no effort to lower their voices or to limit their discussions to times and places where she could not overhear them.

Then she realized that the pair felt no need to keep their plans from her because Vance Harper had assured them she would not be alive to leave the place where they were taking her. The realization was no shock to Jessie. Other men in other gangs had marked her for death, and failed. However, Jessie had learned long ago that she would find out more by listening than by talking, and she kept her facial expression as placid as though she were deaf.

Even when her captors mentioned her name in their speculations and turned to look at her as though they expected her to protest or make some sort of comment about one of their remarks, she ignored their expectant glances, for while Jessie was tucking their comments about Vance Harper into her memory, she was also engaged in speculations of her own.

Although she was certain that Ki would be somewhere close behind, that certainty was all that Jessie had to sustain her belief. The quick glances she'd made over her shoulder from time to time during their largely silent ride from the hotel had shown her only the faint strip of the trail.

After they'd passed through the largely logged-over area near town, the trail had narrowed and grown sinuous. At times, where stretches of stone broke through the surface soil, it became difficult for the horses to keep a sure footing and the men had been forced to move snail-like across the solid rock outcrops. They'd made only one real stop, in a still-untouched stand of small pines, for a meal of crackers and summer sausage, and it had been eaten in the saddle.

When they started moving along the trail again, Jessie noted that in spite of the halt to rest their horses, the animals' pace had not improved. It was actually a bit slower than it had been before they'd stopped. Until that moment, and in spite of her familiarity with horses, Jessie had not realized how much stress had been put on the animals by the long hours of constant plodding over the rugged and mostly uphill trail. Now Jessie began putting her mind to work testing ideas that might help Ki, for she was certain that he must be somewhere behind them.

In spite of the glow that brightened the sky from the top rim of the setting sun, which still showed above the western horizon, dusk's first shades were creeping into the eastern sky when Jessie's captors reined off the barely beaten trail they'd been following and struck off through the pine forest at right angles to the trail.

Jessie could distinguish no great difference between this small spot of shelter and the others where the men had halted, but it was obvious that her captors had been there before. They started toward a thick growth of pines that rose beyond a few scattered stumps, some distance away from the trail.

As they reined toward it, she could see at once that the stand of pines would hide them and their horses from anyone passing on the trail, the gathering gloom of evening having suddenly grown even deeper. A frown formed on Jessie's face as she realized that even a tracker as expert as Ki could not follow her trail in the dark.

Jessie's frown grew even more thoughtful as she glanced at the thongs securing her wrists to her saddle horn. Then she lifted her eyes to watch the men riding ahead of her, at the end of the lead rope that was knotted to the reins of her horse. Bending forward in her saddle, she managed to shift her shoulders sidewise inch by inch until the tips of the knot in her neckerchief brushed her hands.

Flicking her eyes ahead, Jessie could see that the men were paying no attention to her. Their eyes were on the unpredictable ups and downs on the narrow path winding in front of them as they followed its sudden turns, zigzagging toward the stand of pine trees. As stiff as her fingers were, Jessie grasped the knot and worked it loose. She managed to hold tightly to a corner of the neckerchief as she raised herself erect in her saddle again.

Loosening her fingers, she let the bright yellow neckerchief drop to the ground. After her horse had plodded a short distance ahead, Jessie looked back and found that she could still see the light blotch of the kerchief lying beside the trail.

Even before Jessie and her captors turned off the trail, a deepening blue had begun showing in the eastern sky. It spread slowly upward, and as the sky's color changed and the darker blue crawled slowly toward the forests on both sides of the trail, the ground below the pine trees that formed the grove began to become shrouded with the gloom of approaching night.

"It's been a good while since I was along this trail, last," Lem observed after they'd ridden in silence for some time.

"Well, this place ain't changed a bit," Brace told Lem. "But I'm like you—it's been a fair spell since the last time I seen it. And from the way it looks up ahead where there ain't been too much cutting-over, it's just the same that it always was."

"Funny." Lem frowned. "It sorta seems like to me that somebody's been stretching things out a mite, but guess it's on account of me not being in these parts for as long as I have. Are you sure we're still heading right to get to the place where we're supposed to meet up with Harper?"

"Sure as I can be about anything," Brace replied. "We got a pretty good bit of riding left to do before we get to the next stretch of cut-over land, but the old camp ain't too far past the cutover part. I sure don't aim to try crossing through them stumps in the dark, though. I seen

102

too many good horses crippled trying to go across them when they couldn't see them big cracks in the ground and stepped into one of 'em."

"Well, maybe I don't recall things right, but it seems like to me we've come a right good ways from town. Maybe we better push on a mite faster. Harper'll be looking for us to get there before it's plumb dark, and it's getting on to be past my suppertime."

Brace snapped, "Now, just settle down and cut off your griping. My belly thinks my throat's been cut, too, but we got to push on regardless. We sure don't want to lose whatever little bit of daylight that's left. Was we to stop and feed our faces we'd be too pushed to finish eating while there's still enough light left for us to chew by, let alone ride by."

"All right, you're the boss," Lem replied. "I ain't going to do no talking back. I don't aim to get caught out in these cutovers after dark, neither. And the sooner we get this Starbuck dame off our hands, the better I'll like it.

Ki glanced at the sun. It was hanging closer to the horizon now, and its brilliant golden face was taking on a reddish hue. During daylight hours, Ki had been forced to keep a substantial distance from Jessie and the men who'd kidnapped her from the hotel. Even though the road that her captors had taken did not follow the sinuous Mendocino coastline, it was a winding one, even seeming to curve back upon itself at times.

To avoid being seen Ki had taken the precaution of leaving the beaten pathway where it curved and riding in a straight line to the point where the curve ended. Although pushing ahead between the tree trunks meant slower progress as well as a few extra minutes studying the trail when he rejoined it, he lost little time.

Wherever he moved, Ki kept his eyes busy, flicking them from side to side to assure himself that he had not lost sight of the hoofprints he was following, and reined in only on the rare occasions when he reached the top of an upslope. Long ago Ki had learned that the pine forest usually thinned on high ground, and this offered him an opportunity for a better survey of his surroundings.

Now the setting sun was only a short distance above the western horizon. Ahead, beyond a high ridge that was hiding his quarry momentarily, Ki could see that the road sloped sharply upward between a forest of stumps. His field of vision was small, and though he tried to catch a glimpse of Jessie and her captors, he had no success.

Ki was about to turn away and continue in the direction he'd been moving when he noticed the glowing glint of a foreign color on the ground. He had been flicking his eyes quickly from place to place and had already turned his head away from the splash of alien color and was lifting the reins to swing his mount around as well when he realized that he'd been looking at the familiar color of Jessie's bright scarf.

Yanking the horse's reins around, Ki headed for the crumpled cloth. He pulled up and slid off his horse's back to pick up the smooth, brilliant fabric square. Even before he had it in his hand, there was no mistaking the bright silk fabric. Ki stood for a moment, shifting his gaze slowly, and at last caught sight of the barely visible path—too small and faintly marked to be called a trail—that angled off from the direction in which he'd been moving and led through the thick forest of uncut pine trees, and many cut as well.

Now Ki wasted no time. Leading his horse, he plunged into the thick growth of pines. Though the tall uncut trees shaded the hard ground, making it difficult for him to see where the layer of duff on the forest floor had been disturbed, Ki's zigzag moves soon began to pay him a rich dividend. Where the duff lay thickest on the ground and the stumps were spaced closer together, he could see the faint hoofprints more easily, and was able to move faster.

Most of the stumps were only waist-high, but Ki had already noticed how closely-spaced they were, and was reasonably sure that he could count on them as a temporary shelter. He peered ahead, but in the devastated area, the forest of stumps was so thick that he could see little of the land beyond the massive boles of dead trees left standing by the timber cutters. Then, suddenly, and at a distance which Ki could not calculate, a flicker of movement caught his eyes.

Ki stopped at once and swung up into his saddle. From the higher vantage point he looked ahead just in time to see Jessie and her captors. They were silhouetted against the deepening blue of the sky, already giving promise of approaching darkness, as they reached the crest of the long rise and disappeared. Ki began to breathe more easily when he saw Jessie, for soon after its last fork the road's surface had become a claylike soil that took prints readily when wet and few or no prints when it was dry.

Even at a distance, Ki could see the weapons of Jessie's abductors. Each of them wore a hip-holstered revolver in addition to a rifle in a long saddle-sheath. Being outgunned was no novelty to Ki, nor was going single-handed against two antagonists.

Ki wasted no time in self-congratulation for his successful tracking. Instead, he studied the sky for a moment to see how much time would pass before the onset of the full darkness that would be required to cover his moves after he'd caught up with Jessie and her captors. The bottom curve of the reddening sun was below the treetops now, which meant that another hour or perhaps a bit more must pass before he'd be safe in getting any closer to them.

After a moment's thoughtful consideration, Ki decided to gamble that he could keep from being observed if he speeded his pace. He knew that he must move quickly to reach the crest of the long rise ahead, for Jessie and her kidnappers were no longer in sight on the limited section of the road that he could see. Ki dug the toe of his sandal into the horse's flank and the animal picked up its gait.

When Ki reached the crest of the long, gentle slope, he could still see no sign of Jessie and the men who held her as their prisoner. The section of the trail that was visible was limited; it curved beyond a thicker than usual stand of trees, and beyond the treetops Ki could see the crest of another of the high rock outcrops that he'd encountered earlier.

Full darkness was close, Ki was in strange territory, and even from a distance, he could see that the forest ahead rose thickly on both sides of the narrow road. By this time the road had shriveled to little more than a half-visible trail. It no longer ran through a cleared swath of timber, but wove in and out between the trees.

Ki knew that he must close the distance, and do it quickly, no matter what the risk. The rock-hard surface of the trail was a maze of half-visible hoofprints, but few of them were fresh. Confident that he could recognize those made by the horses ridden by Jessie and the two men who'd abducted her and toeing his horse again, he set the animal moving at a faster pace.

"Well, I ain't going to make no bones about being glad to see them shacks up ahead," Lem told Brace. "I ain't forked a horse over such a long stretch of rough ground since I got outa jail this last time. I reckon you're sure it's where we're headed."

As Lem spoke, he was peering through the stand of pines that still separated them from the weatherbeaten gray walls of the scattered group of buildings ahead. They'd just sighted the array of ramshackle structures through the thinning pine forest.

"Oh, it's the right place, all right," Brace replied. "I been here too many times when this camp was running not to know it now."

"Well, it sure didn't take much time to go to hell," Lem observed. "What do you figure a rich man like Vance Harper wants with a mess like this is?"

"I reckon you'll have to ask him that," Brace said. "I just work for him; he don't ever tell me why he wants a job done. It's just like us bringing the Starbuck woman here. He didn't say why he wanted her; he just said grab her and get her here."

Jessie was listening to the exchange between her captors while she made her own examination of the abandoned logging camp. It dwarfed in size the ramshackle remains of the camp where she and Ki had sheltered on their earlier short swing through the redwood stands to the south.

That this camp had at one time been been a busy place was clear to her, for she looked at its weatherbeaten buildings with eyes that had inspected the extensive timber properties she'd inherited from Alex Starbuck.

Clustered loosely together on a stump-dotted arc beside the bank of a small creek Jessie could see the mill's main building and its dining hall as well as a dozen or more one-room shacks. Of the widely varying array, only the main building seemed sturdy enough to be fit for use. It was two stories high, with the second floor projecting over a wide veranda that still had most of an elaborate railing along its outer edge. In many of the windows both on the ground floor and the upper floor panes of glass shone, still unbroken.

All the shacks were in their last stages of collapse; they were little more than crisscrossed heaps of splintered boards and shingles, while the sawmill itself was little more than a framework of wall joists and rafters. Its walls were gone and so were most of the roof's shingles. The saw base still stood, though many of the big stone blocks that had supported the boiler and the saw were cracked and broken. The solid block of stone on which had sat the massive saw itself and the steam engine that provided its power was badly cracked, and both saw and engine had been removed.

Lem and Brace paid no attention to Jessie as they continued leading her horse with them steadily ahead toward the main building. They paid no more attention to her than they had while on the trail. Now as they drew closer to the big structure, the door opened and Vance Harper stepped outside.

He crossed the wide porch and stood motionless for a moment at its hip-high railing, eyeing the approaching riders, a grin forming on his face. Then he stepped down to the ground and waited while they reached him and reined in.

"Well, now," Harper said, "I'll have to give you boys credit for following orders. Did she give you any trouble?"

108

"Just a little bit," Brace said. "But we only had to reason with her a time or two."

"What about the Chink that's traveling with her?" Harper frowned. "I guess you took care of him?"

"Why, he wasn't around at all," Brace replied. "We sure didn't see hide nor hair of him at the hotel, so I reckon we give him the slip."

"Good," Harper said. Turning to Jessie, he went on, "I'm sure you've figured out why these two men brought you here, Miss Starbuck. One way or another, I aim to own this big spread of prime timberland. You've already told me you won't sell out, but in this place where nobody's going to bother me, I figure I'll find a way to persuade you."

Jessie's voice was ice-cool and showed no hint of stress as she said, "I take what you've said to mean that if I keep refusing to sell, which is certainly what I'll do, you'll torture me until I agree to sell?" When Harper did not reply, she went on, "Don't have any illusions about me. I can be very stubborn when someone's trying to force me to do something I have no intention of doing."

"We'll just have to see about that," Harper told her. Turning back to Lem, he went on, "Now, I'll have to step back inside to get the rest of the money I owe you. Just sit still, and soon as I've paid you off you'll be free to get the hell out of Mendocino for good."

Turning, Harper went back into the building. Lem had turned to say something to Brace when the first shot from one of the windows took him. When the lead tore into him he reared back in his saddle and started to sag to the ground. Taken completely by surprise, Brace swept his hand to his holster. Before he could draw, a second shot barked from the building and Brace crumpled, falling

109

backward. The bodies of the two outlaws hit the ground only seconds apart.

Jessie was as completely surprised as the outlaws had been. She made an involuntary effort to move, but her bonds held her motionless. She could only sit in her saddle and stare at the building in horror.

★

Chapter 10

For the fraction of a second following the shot that had toppled Lem, Jessie had been certain that she would become the target of the next chunk of deadly lead. Her feeling of certainty lasted for only a few seconds, until Harper's second shot cracked from within the building. The bullet tore into Brace's chest and knocked him to the ground.

Brace landed only a yard or two from the motionless form of his companion. He managed to lift himself on an elbow and raise his gunhand in the beginning of a draw, but even before the hand was halfway to his holstered revolver, his arm went limp and fell to the ground. A climactic shudder swept through his prone form; then his body twitched a time or two as the total stillness of death claimed him.

Jessie relaxed a bit when no third shot broke the silence that had settled over the big abandoned structure and the area around it. She realized that at least for the moment she was safe, but her mind was working rapidly as she watched the shattered window through which Harper had fired. Its curtains were now billowing out of the glassless bottom sash. Their flutters hid the interior of the room beyond, and she could see no signs of movement inside.

Harper's cold-blooded murder of Lem and Brace had told Jessie two things. First, Harper had only one reason to kill the outlaws he'd hired to kidnap her: dead men could never testify against him in case he was tried for having her abducted.

Jessie's second conclusion followed quickly on the heels of her first: Harper would not be likely to harm her as long as she held the keys on which the success of his schemes depended.

During the few moments while Jessie sat motionless, she twisted in her saddle a bit to look along the trail that led from the expansive pine forest, hoping to catch sight of Ki. She saw only the trees beyond the clearing, their branches swaying gently in the light breeze that had cleared away the gunsmoke.

When Harper emerged from the building, he was carrying a rifle, obviously the weapon he'd used to cut down Lem and Brace. He stopped on the wide veranda, his eyes fixed on Jessie. She did not speak or move, but sat silently in her saddle, motionless, waiting for him to take the initiative. She flicked her eyes away from him as he walked a few steps and stopped at the veranda's wide, hip-high railing.

Resting the butt of the rifle on the veranda's rail and leaning forward toward Jessie, he stared fixedly at her. Harper's small, obsidian-black eyes reminded her of the chilling stare of a coiled rattlesnake about to strike its prey.

"I hope you're not too upset by that little fracas you just seen, Miss Starbuck," he said.

112

His voice held no hint of an apology, but Jessie had not expected one. She did not reply while Harper inspected the two sprawled corpses on the ground, but she did not turn her head away from him.

Now Harper went on. "You've got to understand that those men knew too much about my business and what I've been doing, and about the plans I've got. I couldn't afford to let them go on living, knowing as much as they did."

Jessie's voice was icicle-cold as she replied, "After what I've just seen, I'm sure you don't expect me to believe that you'd ever let me go free, knowing as much as I do."

"Why, you've got nothing to worry about," Harper assured her. Then he quickly modified his statement by adding, "At least not right now. You and me've got some unfinished business to take care of."

Her voice dripping sarcasm, Jessie asked, "And you don't intend to murder me until we finish it?"

"Now if you're as smart a lady as I take you to be, you'd know that killing you would be a fool's trick. What I'm looking to do is make a business deal with you. I'd have to be a plumb damn jackass to kill you."

"And I'd be a bigger jackass if I even considered doing any business with you, after what I've seen in the past few minutes," Jessie said. She kept her voice level, suppressing her anger.

"Maybe so and maybe no," Harper told her. "But I got a pretty good idea you'll come around to dealing with me."

"I'm sure you won't think it's strange if I find that hard to believe," Jessie told him.

"Folks change their minds all the time. What I aim to do right now is give you a few things to think about that might help you change yours about doing business the way I intend to have it done."

"Save your breath!" Jessie snapped. She stopped short, realizing that anger was no answer to Harper's threats.

"Oh, I got plenty of breath to use and still have a lot left over. And after you think on it a while you just might come to see things my way. There's all sorts of ugly tricks that I can use to make you change your mind."

"I've listened to threats like that before," Jessie replied. She kept her anger from being reflected in her voice. "Yours don't upset me any more than others have."

"What I've said up until now's just for starters," Harper told her. "But if you'd like for me to help you think straight, I'll be glad to give you a few ideas about some of the ways I can think of to make a stubborn woman change her mind."

"How you start or how you finish, or how many threats you make, you'll find that I'm not going to change my mind," Jessie replied. She resolved to keep playing for time as long as Harper would allow her to. She went on, "And just because I'm a woman doesn't mean that you can either frighten me or talk me into doing something I have no intention to do."

"Well, I was hoping you'd save me a lot of trouble by being obliging, but like I said, I'll start easy and give you plenty of time to think things over," Harper said. "Except that there's one thing you better understand. I've got my mind made up to get hold of every stand of timberland here in Mendocino. And that includes your land, whether you own it or lease it. And I'll have everything you got here, like your mill and whatever else there is."

Jessie was beginning to wonder if she could sustain her time-consuming efforts long enough to give Ki a chance to reach her. She said, "I'm sure you realize that

I'm not at all impressed by your threats."

Harper was obviously puzzled by the calmness in Jessie's tone. The menace in his voice matched that of his threatening frown as he said, "They better bother you, lady, because I'm not just talking so I can hear myself. And you better do what I want you to. If you don't, I got a lot of tricks you ain't likely to've run into. Like having the end of a red-hot poker put a few stripes on them pretty cheeks of yours."

"I've had other outlaws threaten to do that," Jessie told him. "But you don't see any scars on my face."

"Oh, that's not the only trick I got," Harper assured her. "Maybe you'd listen better if I tied your legs spraddled out and jammed a good-sized log up into you. I never have run across a woman yet who could hold out against that."

"I'm sure—" Jessie broke off as the shining arc of Ki's *shuriken* cut through the air a short distance from her head and buried itself in Harper's shoulder.

Yowling with pain, Harper let his rifle clatter to the floor and brought up both hands to grasp the embedded throwing blade. Blood began flowing from his palms as he tried to work the blade out of his shoulder. He had not succeeded in freeing it when hoofbeats thunked from the trees beyond the strip of cleared land that separated them from the building.

Jessie had known what to do the instant she'd seen the silvery arc of the *shuriken* sail past her and cut into Harper. She turned away from him in time to see Ki galloping toward her across the cleared land.

Harper was still tugging at the *shuriken* that was embedded in his shoulder. He heard and saw Ki and dropped to his knees on the floor of the veranda, reaching for the rifle that had tumbled from his hand. Ki had drawn his *do* by the time he reached Jessie.

115

He slashed away her bonds with the long, slim blade of the *do* and twisted in his saddle to glance at the veranda.

"Ride, Jessie!" Ki said. "Get behind what's left of the old sawmill. I'll catch up with you."

Jessie turned toward Ki, but he was already dropping off his horse, and she knew him well enough to realize that he was going to cover her escape. Knowing the futility of arguing with Ki when he placed himself between her and danger, Jessie thunked her boot heels into the flanks of her mount but at the same time called to him.

"Ki! Don't try to go against Harper! He's already wounded, but he's still dangerous! Get on your horse and come with me!"

Ki turned his head to look at Harper and saw that the wounded man had started crawling toward his rifle. Ki's hand went to the case on his forearm that held his *shuriken*. Even while he was reaching for the case, he saw that the blade would be wasted, for at the angle he'd be forced to launch his throw, the blade would almost certainly be deflected by the slats supporting the porch railing.

Ki also realized that before he could get to the rail of the veranda, Harper would succeed in retrieving his rifle, for now it was only inches from his outstretched hand. Reacting instantly to the changed situation, he abandoned his first plan. Leaping into the saddle of his horse, Ki prodded it with his sandaled toe and wheeled it around to follow Jessie.

She had almost reached the high, massive block of crumbling concrete that had been the sawmill's foundation. Turning in her saddle, Jessie saw Ki following her and pulled up to wait for him. When he reached her side, they galloped together toward the shelter of the abandoned mill.

They'd covered all but a few yards of the short distance to their goal before Harper got his hands on his rifle. Rising to his knees, he shouldered the rifle in spite of his wound and fired at them. It was a hurried shot, and the rifle's bullet did no more harm than raising a puff of dirt just ahead of Jessie's horse. The animal shied but did not break stride.

Before Harper could trigger off another round, Jessie and Ki had turned their mounts around the corner of the massive block of concrete and stone that had supported the sawmill's machinery. The old foundation rose high enough above the ground to shelter them, even on horseback. They circled it until they reached a spot where they'd be out of Harper's sight as well as where his bullets could not reach them. Then they reined in to give their panting horses a chance to breathe.

"We won't be safe here very long," Jessie said. "Harper's going to be watching for us if we move out into the open. He's not going let us get away if he can help it."

"He's already proved that," Ki agreed.

He stood up in his stirrups, rising slowly to be sure his head would not be visible to Harper. Balancing himself in the stirrups, Ki first scanned the broad expanse of open ground that stretched from the ruins of the sawmill to the nearest stands of pine trees, then turned to look for any signs of movement in the direction of the ruins of the mill camp. There was no sign of life or movement in any direction.

"Whatever we do, we've got to keep this big chunk of concrete between us and Harper," Ki told Jessie as he dropped back into his saddle. "There's no place I can see for us to move to except those wrecked shanties, and they wouldn't give us enough shelter to be useful. And the river's just beyond them."

"Harper's probably looking in that direction, anyhow," Jessie said. "He'd expect us to start for the timber. But if we were to split up and—" Stopping short, Jessie shook her head. "No, Ki. I thought it might be a good idea, but it wouldn't work either."

"We can't afford to underestimate Harper," Ki went on. "When he's had time to think for a minute or two he'll be coming after us."

"We'll just have to go the other way, then," Jessie said.

She gestured toward the broken ground beyond the concrete barrier. It was a seemingly endless expanse of logged-over pine forest, the stumps of trees that had been felled in past years rising waist-high from the stone-pocked soil. Most of the stumps were huge, larger in diameter than a big man's shoulders.

Many of the stumps were now sprouting fresh growths of finger-sized branches only a little higher than a man's head. These were covered with short green twigs, which had sprouted needles of an even darker green. Between the stumps the ground was hidden by the centuries-old carpet created by the shedding of pine needles, with added layers of sawdust deposited by the mill during its years of operation.

Most of the needles were dead and ranged in color from the pale yellow of those that had fallen years ago to a mellow tan. They were only a few shades darker than the patches of sandy soil that showed in a few places where the huge boles of pines felled in years past were spaced far apart.

After Jessie had glanced toward the remains of what

had been a huge stretch of pine forest, she turned back to Ki.

"It looks like we don't have much choice," she said. "But if—"

Ki broke in. He said, "Those stumps are big enough to give us the kind of cover we need, Jessie. And unless Harper's good at tracking we can hide our horses' hoofprints by zigzagging between them. We're bound to make some noise, but that can't be helped."

"I don't like to run from trouble, Ki." Jessie frowned. "And Harper probably knows the lay of the land here a lot better than we do, since he's been looking at it with the idea of buying it."

"Of course he knows the land better than we do," Ki agreed. "But if we leave right now, we'll probably be able to stay ahead of him until we come to a place that will give us better cover. And we're bound to cross some stony stretches where he'll have trouble keeping on our trail."

"You know what Alex used to say," Jessie said. "The longer you put off facing trouble, the bigger the trouble grows. We might be better off just waiting here for Harper to come looking for us. It would be a quick showdown, and—"

"I won't argue that with you," Ki replied. "But except for the five or six *shuriken* that are left in my pouch, we don't have any weapons. Harper's got his rifle, and I'm sure he'll have a pistol tucked away somewhere in his gear. We can't put up a very good fight if he should catch up with us."

Jessie did not reply for a moment; then she said, "We haven't heard a sound from Harper yet. He's probably putting a bandage on that wound you gave him with your *shuriken*."

"Or packing his saddlebags, getting ready to ride after us," Ki suggested.

"Possibly," she agreed. "but we've been here a long time. The sooner we move, the better. Let's get started, Ki. When we see the right place to stop, we'll know it and hole up, and take our chances of Harper finding us."

"You didn't mention the other possibility, Jessie," Ki told her.

"Perhaps not, but I thought about it," she said. "You mean for us to attack Harper here, before he comes looking for us?"

"It might be the last move he'd be expecting."

"I'll grant you that, Ki." Jessie nodded. "But do you really think it's practical, you with so few *shuriken* and me with no weapons at all?"

"We've been in worse situations," Ki reminded her.

"Of course," she agreed. "But so far we've managed to stay a bit ahead of him, and until we can do something to even the odds between us and him by even a little bit, I'd be inclined to say that the more distance we can keep from him the better."

"Then let's start moving," Ki suggested.

"I've been thinking that we can circle around the old office building and head back to Mendocino City. What's your idea?"

"We'll have to head back there sooner or later," Ki said. "And I'd bet that's what Harper will think of first, just as we did. My guess is that he'll be planning to hide along the trail and ambush us."

"Then we won't take the trail," Jessie said. "We'll angle off through the forest and pick it up after we've gotten several miles from here."

"We don't often disagree, Jessie," Ki told her. "But

120

I'm against traveling on that trail to Mendocino City. If we take it, we'll just be Harper's sitting ducks."

"What's your suggestion, then?"

"Lay down a false trail through that big stand of pine that will give him the idea we're going to head for Mendocino City," Ki said. "Somewhere along the way we'll be sure to run into a stretch of rock or hard ground that will hide our tracks. That's when we'll double back and follow Harper into Mendocino City. Once we get there, our troubles with him are over."

"It sounds good to me," Jessie agreed. "Let's get into the shelter of those pines, then we can circle around the old office building and lay down our false trail for Harper."

Ki nodded. They turned their horses away from the huge block of concrete and brick that had been their shelter and started through the stump forest.

Chapter 11

"There's that noise again, Ki!" Jessie exclaimed. As she spoke, Jessie reined in and Ki pulled his horse up beside hers. She went on, "And I still can't tell where it came from any more than I could the first time we heard it. Did you manage to figure it out?"

"No more than you did, Jessie," Ki replied. "It could be just ahead of us, or it could have come from either side of us, but not from behind."

"It's the way these long shoots are growing from the stumps," she went on. "Somehow they seem to scatter the sound."

Jessie and Ki had been winding in and out between the hip-high pine stumps of the huge stand for what seemed to them an endless amount of time. They'd abandoned making a false trail because they could see that leaving one was difficult in these woods, and they were mostly sure that Harper couldn't follow what they'd left.

Unlike bare earth, the duff—a thick layer of pine needles and small twigs on the soil—would not take the clear impression of a man's booted foot or an animal's paw or hoof. They'd been forced to zigzag from one to another of the short stretches of tall crowns of fresh green shoots sprouting from the tops and sides of the stumps, searching the faint trail without success.

Occasionally, for the past mile or so and at very long intervals, a light gust of the unpredictable breeze had been carrying strange sounds to their ears. The noises could have been the distant, muffled reverberations of a horse's hooves or only the bumping together of the intertwining shoots that rose from the tree stumps.

Each time they'd heard one of the alien sounds, Jessie and Ki had exchanged questioning glances, thinking of Vance Harper. When they'd reined in and tried to locate the direction from which the faint thumps were coming, either the sounds had stopped or the fitful shifting breeze had changed its course.

As they moved steadily away from the abandoned logging camp the unidentifiable sounds continued to break the forest's stillness now and then. Hearing them, Jessie and Ki agreed that they might be hearing a deer or bear instead of Vance Harper's horse's hooves on the coarse soil underfoot. The faint raspings and rustles that reached their ears were still too light and too distant for them to identify with any certainty. Their horses were beginning to tire, so they pulled up beside a larger than usual cluster of stumps to give the animals a few minutes' rest.

For a moment they sat silently in their saddles, trying to interpret the whispered stirrings carried to them by the breeze. When no new or different noises reached them, Jessie turned to Ki and said, "I'm sure we agree that we're still a long way from finding out where those odd noises are coming from."

"I feel exactly as you do," Ki replied. "And we don't have much more daylight left."

"That's what I've been thinking," Jessie agreed. "But if Harper's trying to follow us, which I don't think he is now, he's going to be forced to give up before too long. Wouldn't you say it's about time we stopped for the night?"

"We'll be a lot better off if we stop before it gets too dark for us to pick out a good spot," Ki suggested.

Jessie nodded agreement, then said, "If I'm not mistaken, I can see a place like the one we're looking for. It's right ahead there, where the trail curves."

As she spoke, she was gesturing toward the path in front of them, now only faintly visible in the dying light. Ki's eyes followed the motion of her hand. Straining to make out details in the steadily deepening dusk, he saw that they were about to enter a stretch of the trail that was beginning to curve around a small stand of trees.

When Ki studied the spot, he could see that it was much like others they'd passed after leaving the shelter of the ruined sawmill's foundation. Just off the trail a growth of young pine branches had sprouted upward from the massive stumps of older trees that had been felled years ago. The original trees had grown in a rough circle around a clear stretch of ground, and the fresh growth, which had already risen high above most of the stumps, was thicker than any they'd encountered so far.

"Perhaps it's even a little bit better than some of the other places we've seen," Ki told Jessie as he turned back to her. "It's shielded, so the wind won't bother us too much. We aren't likely to be noticed from the trail, and at the same time we'll be able to see everything around us."

"Which just might save us from being surprised by Harper, if he's still managing to follow us," Jessie went on.

"That's something we still can't be sure of, Jessie. All we've heard has been a few faint noises, and if it is Harper who made them, we've never managed to catch sight of him," Ki pointed out. "But with night as close as it is to settling in, he might have just given up looking for us."

"That certainly wouldn't bother me," Jessie told him. "We were lucky to get away without having any more of a face-down with Harper than we did."

"And there's sure to be another one, Jessie." Ki frowned. "Either here or when we get back to Mendocino City."

"Oh, of course," Jessie agreed. Her voice was undisturbed as she added, "From what we've seen of Harper, it's quite likely that he'll feel he's got to find us. He knows only too well that we're the only witnesses who can testify against him if he goes to trial for killing those two men so cold-bloodedly. He can't just let us go free after what we've seen."

"Given a little more luck, we might be able to get back to Mendocino City and force him to look for us there," Ki said.

"Better there than here," Jessie said.

They'd been studying their immediate surroundings more closely while they chatted, and had satisfied themselves that the thick layer of duff between the tree roots around the place where they'd stopped bore no signs of fresh hoofprints or footprints. In the limited distance they could scan ahead there were very few breaks in the pine forest's screen.

Through the swiftly waning daylight in these slits of lesser dimness, Jessie and Ki could see that the tops of the massive stubs of pine boles rising just ahead of them were almost level with the backs of their horses. The new growth of branches that had sprouted from the thick stumps jutted almost vertically from the tree trunks. The shoots were higher than the heads of both Jessie and Ki, even though they were still on horseback. They formed an unusually dense screen, hiding the land ahead.

After listening for a few minutes longer, and standing up in their stirrups once more to take a final look around, Jessie and Ki exchanged nods of satisfaction. They dismounted, then led their horses off the trail and into the little sheltered clearing, where they busied themselves in preparation to settle down for the night.

Their chores were very simple. After tethering their mounts at one side of the little open area and unsaddling, they moved to the opposite side of the small clearing. There they spread the saddle blankets on the ground. The strong aroma of horse sweat carried by their improvised bedding bothered them for only a few moments. Even before the deepest blackness of night had finished closing down around them, Jessie and Ki had pulled the blankets up to their ears to shield themselves against the chilling, fitful night breeze.

Their day had been long and arduous; being able to relax fully for the first time after so many strenuous hours brought both Jessie and Ki a feeling of relief as well as a sense of security. Sleep claimed them almost at once.

Jessie's eyes suddenly snapped open. Subconsciously, she was aware that some sort of alien sound had broken her sleep, but for the first few seconds after she'd wakened in the darkness, she could see nothing. She lay motionless for a few moments and blinked her eyes a time or two as she turned her head slowly from side to side. Gradually, aided by the patches of moonlight that now flooded the forest, she got her night vision.

During the time Jessie and Ki had been sleeping the moon had risen high. Though the lower portion of the patch of eastern sky, which Jessie had glimpsed when she first opened her eyes, was showing a suggestion of oncoming daybreak in its fading blue, the stars were still brilliant directly overhead.

Jessie glanced up at the declining moon, the golden hue of its face seeming to be crisscrossed with a maze of tiny lines. Then she realized that the lines were silhouettes formed against the moon by the fresh living shoots that were growing from the stumps of the felled trees that thrust up around the clearing.

Gradually, as her eyes grew accustomed to the liquid darkness, Jessie could make out Ki's recumbent form a short distance away. His bedroll was a rumpled rectangular blob, its dark brown blankets swallowing the shadows that dappled the ground around them. Across the little clearing, Jessie found that she was also able to see the dark, bulking outlines of their tethered horses. She tried to look beyond them, but the stumps from which the tall shoots grew so thickly blocked her view of the trail.

Jessie was about to settle back into her bedroll and resume her interrupted sleep when a beam of moonlight suddenly appeared where there had been no moonshine visible before. For a moment she thought it was caused by the wind stirring a stray branch shooting up from one of the stumps. Then she realized that there'd been no breeze to stir it.

"Ki!" Jessie whispered, trying to pitch her voice so low that it could be heard only a short distance. "I just saw one of those tree shoots move when there wasn't any wind to move it!"

"Where?" Ki asked, his whisper no louder than Jessie's.

"Toward the trail beyond me and on my right side."

Ki moved then. Jessie could see him rising from his blankets and hunkering down beside them. She was not sure how clearly Ki could see her in the darkness; she lifted her arm a bit and wriggled her fingers to draw his attention.

"I can see your hand, Jessie," Ki whispered. "Now tell me whether the movement you saw was to your left or your right."

"A bit to the left, Ki. Not much, just a few inches."

Ki shifted his eyes in the direction Jessie had indicated. For a few moments he saw nothing but a few of the high tree shoots quivering in the faint breeze. Then in one spot the branches, silhouetted against the night sky, stirred and separated a bit before suddenly snapping back into their original position.

"Someone or something's prowling in here," Ki told Jessie. His whisper was barely loud enough to reach her ears.

"That's what I think, too," Jessie replied. Her voice was pitched as low as Ki's. "But it's so dark down here on the ground that I can't see what or who it is."

"There's only one way to find out," Ki told her. "You stay here. I'll work my way along the ground and try to get close enough to find out."

Jessie did not argue against his suggestion; she knew that she could not match the silence and stealth in moving about that Ki's *ninjitsu* training had taught him. His figure was visible to her only during the few moments required for him to disappear in the gloom. She watched his silent movements as he started to creep forward, but in the forest of stumps she soon lost sight of his dark moving form.

Neither Jessie nor Ki was prepared for the eerie shriek that broke the silence a moment or two after Ki had begun his darkness shrouded advance. It was a ululating cry that might have burst from the throat of a wounded animal or from a human in some threat or in an agony of terrible pain. Its throbbing hung in the still night air and almost drowned the muffled thud of running footsteps that reached their ears as the cry died away.

Jessie hesitated for only a moment while she weighed the wisdom of calling to Ki. Then, as the echoes of the strange shriek died away, she realized that whatever or whoever had loosed the eerie cry was running instead of attacking.

"Ki?" she called. "Are you all right?"

"Of course," he replied. "Don't move yet, though. And don't make any noise. I couldn't see who or what that was, but whatever I saw was a lot bigger than both of us put together."

"You did see something, though?" Jessie asked as she saw Ki silhouetted against the night sky, coming toward her across the little clearing.

"Oh, it was something, all right," Ki replied. "And a very big something, too. I'd say it was at least as big as the largest bear I've ever seen."

"You're sure it wasn't a bear?"

"You know that bears don't run on their hind legs, Jessie," Ki replied.

"You mean it was a man? A person?" she asked.

Ki could not see Jessie's frown in the darkness, but he knew from the pitch of her voice that a frown was on her face. As he reached her side, he said, "I'm not sure what it was, Jessie. All I got was a glimpse of a big form moving away."

Jessie was silent for a moment or two; then she said, "I suppose all that we can do is wait for daybreak, Ki. It'll be another half hour, maybe even longer, before the sky will brighten."

"You go back to your bedroll, then," Ki told Jessie. "I'll circle around a little bit. Whatever the thing we saw was, it might've stopped somewhere close by."

"But it's still too dark for you to see anything, Ki," Jessie objected. "Not even if you're close to whatever you might be trying to look at."

"I'll be listening instead of looking," Ki said. "If whatever it was we saw kept on moving, I'll hear it and try to get close enough to see it, even in the dark."

"Well, I'll be listening, too," Jessie assured him. "I'd say that I'll be looking out, but as dense as these shoots are and as dark as it is, I'm not any too certain that I'll be able to see anything further than an arm's length away."

"That's the boat we're both in." Ki nodded. "But all we can do right now is try."

He turned and started across the little clearing. Even though there were no tall trees to cast dark shadows, the stars in the moonless sky shed so little light that Ki was compelled to move much more slowly than he'd have liked. He knew that the trail he and Jessie had followed earlier was somewhere close, but though he strained his eyes as he moved in a series of wide zigzags, he could make out nothing from his efforts to inspect the ground.

Now and then he stopped and hunkered down, shifting his head slowly from side to side, but his usually keen vision could not penetrate the blackness. He guided

131

himself as well as possible by glancing up at the stars now and then to get their help in keeping his course straight.

Even moving as slowly as he was forced to do, Ki's steady progress had taken him a good distance from the little clearing where he and Jessie had bedded down when he heard a sudden soft scuffing of feet in the distance behind him. He turned quickly, straining to hear well enough to interpret the faint noises, and stood motionless until the silence was broken by a sudden shout that, although muffled, was still audible.

"Ki!" he heard Jessie call. "Something's got hold—"

At that point Jessie's cry was cut off and only a distant susurrus of feet scraping in the duff broke the waning night's stillness.

★

Chapter 12

Ki did not waste a moment. He turned and started back to the clearing where he and Jessie had been sleeping. Before he'd taken more than three or four quick steps, he heard the soft whispers of shuffling feet disturbing the duff in the distance. When he first heard the faint sounds, Ki was sure that the noises were those of an exploring bear.

Stopping to listen, Ki tried to locate the source of the small noises, but in the before-dawn blackness he could see only a few feet in any direction. All that he could be sure of was that the sounds were coming from someplace ahead of him. He could not judge how far away they were; nor could he determine the exact direction from which they came.

Before the almost inaudible and unidentifiable whispers could fade away, Ki resumed his advance. He'd taken only a few steps when the muffled rustlings died suddenly. Again Ki stopped to listen, hoping they would start again and last long enough to give him a chance to relocate them.

After he'd waited a few moments, straining all nerves and turning his head from side to side, the noises resumed. They were not as loud as before. Now they could be heard only as an under-murmur to a sudden burst of distant, solid thunkings that broke through the continuing soft rattle of disturbed undergrowth.

This time it was easier for Ki to separate the noises, and he began trying to identify them. He knew Jessie must be in here somewhere, but where? After a few moments he became convinced that the rustlings were made by somebody—was it Jessie?—pushing through the growth that enclosed the little clearing where he and Jessie had bedded down. He recognized the barely audible, occasional light thuds he was hearing as footsteps or hoofbeats on the hard ground, but they were so faint that Ki could make out no recognizable rhythm or pattern. Had they been Jessie's footsteps, he knew that he would have recognized them at once.

Ki reached a spot where the high tree stumps were spaced far apart and there were fewer thin, whippy shoots than usual rising from them. Now he began to increase his pace a bit as he wove through the growth that lay between the vestiges of the trail and the opening in the forest of stumps where he and Jessie had bedded down. He'd taken only a few steps before he saw a dark form moving ahead of him. A quick glance convinced him that it was a bear, walking on its hind feet instead of on all fours.

No stranger to bears after his many trips with Alex Starbuck into Alaskan regions where bears outnumbered humans and ruled as monarchs of the forest, Ki did not hesitate. He began stamping his feet on the springy layer of pine needles that covered the ground; then he loosed a few loud shouts before beginning to run noisily toward the animal.

As he'd expected, the creature growled, but almost at once it turned and began lumbering away. Its feet made small scratching noises in the duff for a few moments before it disappeared into the darkness and Ki lost sight of it. He stopped and waited. In a few moments the muffled scuffing of its feet was audible again for a few seconds; then the rasping of its paws died away. Ki continued to wait for a moment before resuming his own progress. When he moved ahead again he walked slowly in a pattern of shallow arcs, circling away from the whuffing and muted growls until he could no longer hear them.

Ki continued to zigzag as he peered ahead, but in the starlight each of the small clear spaces that opened between the sawed-off tree trunks looked alike. At last he recognized the bulky forms of his horse and Jessie's tethered in the enclosure. He covered the last few feet, and the entire clearing became visible.

Through the dimness Ki could now see the outlines of their horses even more clearly than before, but there was no sign of Jessie; nor was there any movement in the small dell or in the thick brush around it. He stood in silence for a moment, but now none of the faint rustling noises he'd heard on the patchwork of the trail reached his ears.

"Jessie!" he called. "Jessie! Where are you? Which way are you moving?"

Ki stood in total silence while he waited for a reply, and the stillness of the waning night remained unbroken. For a moment, he stood motionless, weighing the choices he faced. Darkness was his chief enemy now; it figured more commandingly than did time. Glancing at the sky,

Ki saw in the eastward arc of the heavens an almost imperceptible fading of its deep blue hue, a promise that dawn was near.

During the course of his years of service with Alex, followed by the long period of working with Jessie, Ki had learned that moving without a plan wasted time and effort. Forcing himself to be patient, he settled down on his bedroll to wait for the light to improve still further.

Taking advantage of the unforeseen opportunity, Ki busied his mind with planning the moves he must make. He'd barely begun to concentrate when the distant scraping of feet on the hard ground brought his planning to a close.

Jumping to his feet, Ki started swiveling around, turning on his heels as his eyes flicked from side to side as well as up and down. No matter in which direction he looked, he saw nothing but darkness on the land, bright stars dotting the deep blue sky, and outlined against it the black lines of the thin, upshooting second-growth sprigs.

When Ki turned his eyes toward the ground, he could see the tops of the tree stumps and their cylindrical forms for a very short space immediately around him. Beyond there was only blackness. Then, as he kept his eyes busy in spite of his growing feeling of frustration, Ki was sure that he could glimpse a large formless object almost as black as the darkness itself moving slowly among the tree stumps on the opposite side of the clearing.

Ki moved quickly again. He was suddenly concerned that the moving figure might turn toward the blackness shrouding the opposite side of the little clearing. Ki moved silently, his sandaled feet making only a whisper of noise as he advanced. The black form was moving equally slowly, approaching Ki at an angle.

Suddenly Ki's foot slipped on a large, slick branch of a tree that had been lying under the duff across the path he'd elected to take. In spite of his agile moves as he tried to keep his balance, Ki's sliding foot sent him lurching to the ground. He landed with a thud on the layer of soft duff.

Ahead of him the black shadow let out a whuffing snarl. Then above a string of small threatening noises Ki also heard the muted rasping of feet scrabbling through the duff. The black blob disappeared almost at once, but the scraping of its paws or feet was audible long after the almost invisible outlines of its form had been swallowed in the gloom.

Ki was half-sure by now that he'd stumbled onto a black bear roaming in search of a predawn breakfast. He got to his feet and stood motionless for a few moments listening to the diminishing noises of the fleeing animal that he'd surprised. Then the realization grew that if Jessie were anywhere between the bear and his own position, the animal would not have started to approach him. It would have shunned the vicinity of the clearing when human scent reached its sensitive nose.

Never one to hesitate about reaching a decision, Ki made up his mind quickly. His experience had carried two messages. One was that the animal would not have been in the area unless it had been attracted by the food remaining in the horses' saddlebags. The other was that had Jessie and her mysterious abductor been anywhere close by, their human scent would have caused the bear to avoid the area.

Ki knew it would be frustratingly futile to make any more efforts to follow Jessie's faint trail until the light was better. With that unpleasant fact accepted, he settled down at the base of one of the tall stumps and leaned back against it. He closed his eyes, but did not go into a deep sleep. Between moments of fitful dozing, he set himself to thinking, working out the best way to start his search for Jessie when daylight arrived.

Jessie was not certain of anything for several moments after her attempt to call Ki had been smothered by the massive hand of whoever had seized her. The hand covered her face almost completely. She could see a bit through one eye, but even that vision was restricted to a crack between the first and middle fingers of the huge hand.

Jessie's lips were pressed tightly together by the heel of its leathery palm, which was almost as broad as her face and big enough to span it from chin to brow. Its fingers were long enough and big enough to curve around Jessie's forehead and cover her eyes. Her captor's other arm was wrapped around her torso, holding her aside of his own huge body while her arms were trapped tightly against the bottom of her rib-cage.

Jessie's surprise at her sudden capture lasted only for a few fleeting seconds. She started to struggle, trying to force her upper arms away from her body where they were so closely pinioned. Her efforts to loosen the binding pressure of the big arm that was wrapped around her were as futile as they would have been if her entire torso had been circled with loops of stout rope.

Belatedly then, Jessie realized that her legs were free. She began flailing them in a series of stacatto kicks. The toes of her boots met only thin air, but she could feel her heels landing solidly and hear the thunks they made when they hit the legs of whoever or whatever had seized her. Although she'd been certain that her barrage of kicks would bring at least a grunt or some other indication of pain from her captor, the kicks drew no more response than had her efforts to free her arms.

After a moment Jessie stopped kicking and twisting and squirming, for she realized now that she would need to conserve all her energy. Her captor had already proved his strength. Now he continued to prove it by throwing her down and wrapping a cloth around her forehead and pulling it down to cover her eyes as he tightened it and knotted its ends.

Blinded and helpless, Jessie forced herself to remain motionless while enormously large fingers moved along her arms and tightened the bonds around her wrists. Then she became aware of the brushing of the big fingers adjusting the blindfold that cut off her vision, and a moment later she felt the pressure of a gag that sealed her lips. When she tried to speak, the only noise she was able to make was a muffled, meaningless grunting. Even more helpless than before, she did not struggle as she felt the pressure of the thongs binding her arms grow tighter.

Thoroughly trussed and more than a little exhausted, Jessie now felt herself lifted and draped like a meal sack across one of the giant's shoulders. Then the thunking of his feet sounded on the ground as he started moving once more. He walked in giant strides, as though her weight offered him a problem as trivial as her earlier efforts to free herself from his grasp.

Even though she'd struggled fiercely, Jessie's attempts to break free had tired her very little. Her first futile efforts had only strengthened her resolve to liberate herself from the massive arm of her captor. However, at the moment her arms were little better than useless.

Her legs offered even less help than her arms, for when she churned them, trying to kick whoever or whatever was carrying her, she was now simply flailing her feet in empty air. Jessie decided to quit struggling for the moment. She let her tense muscles relax, assuring herself that there would be some time in the future when whatever was carrying her would have to ease the pressure of her bonds and release her. And she knew with certainty by now that she must wait until that moment to make her next effort to break free.

Riding his livery horse and leading Jessie's, Ki started from the clearing as soon as the first pale streaks of dawn light appeared in the eastern sky. The light had not yet reached the stump forest, but Ki did not let the gloom delay his start. He had the confidence common to expert trackers that he could not only discover the most difficult trails, but could follow them to their end.

Gazing ahead through the forest of stumps, Ki began reining his horse in a wide, zigzagging course, letting the animal set its own gait while he gave his full attention to scanning each inch of the deep duff that covered the ground.

There were enough footprints and hoofprints to keep him busy trying to separate the old prints from the new, and there was very little difference between the two kinds. Though his progress was slow, thanks to the constantly brightening sky and the skill in tracking he'd acquired during his long association with Alex and Jessie, he had little difficulty in reading the prints that showed on the deeply marked ground.

From his visits to logging stands through the years, Ki could interpret almost unerringly even the very faintest prints. He recognized easily the most common of the footprints, those made by the calk boots worn by timber cutters, but all that he saw were old prints. Though their impressions were everywhere on the ground, most of them crisscrossed in the ridged soil between the stumps and were blurred by the browned and rotting needles on the ground's surface.

Ki began concentrating his attention on the few fresh prints. He knew that Jessie's custom-made boots had no duplicates anywhere. The prints made by them occurred only at intervals, indicating that she was alternately walking and being carried bodily by whatever had captured her. What drew Ki's attention first and troubled him the most was the strange set of footprints that often appeared superimposed over Jessie's.

These prints seemed to challenge him to identify them, for they were impressions such as Ki had not encountered before. No man that Ki had ever tracked before had worn boots or shoes of such size. There was no mistaking them, for the depressions they'd left were almost as long as Ki's forearm from wrist to elbow and were half as wide as they were long. Wherever the soil was soft, the prints were pressed deeply into the ground.

It was obvious to Ki that whatever had left the prints had no fear of being followed. While this made him wonder a bit about the carelessness of Jessie's captor, it gave Ki no ideas as to his identity or the reason why he should be so thoughtless. He could only draw his conclusions from the evidence of the prints; their depth and their spacing were his only clues.

Jessie learned quickly that while her struggles only induced the giant who was carrying her to tighten his hold on her, she could succeed in making minor moves that eased her discomfort at being handled and carried like an over-filled flour sack.

She continued her cautious wriggling between intervals of motionlessness until she felt reasonably comfortable and the huge strides of the creature no longer jarred her so greatly. She'd managed to relax for a few instants now and then when her captor slowed and zigzagged back and forth. After the first few times he'd done so, Jessie had realized that the silent giant was following a very crooked trail, or had lost some trail he was trying to follow.

For quite some time now, however, whatever was carrying her had been moving without hesitation and taking even longer strides than he had during the first moments after he'd captured her. When he suddenly veered, the swaying of Jessie's body told her that they were now moving in a fresh direction. For several minutes he moved with a quicker step, and when at last he stopped and lowered her to the ground Jessie realized that they must have reached their destination.

Although Ki was far from being satisfied with the progress he was making, he knew that he would be foolish to move faster. There had been two occasions since he'd set out when he had indeed lost sight of the faint signs that he was counting on to guide him. Now, the sky in the east was a bright, red-streaked pink, and the deep blue of the vault above him was beginning to take on a lighter hue.

Ki welcomed the oncoming daylight, for it seemed to him that days instead of hours must have passed since he'd begun his slow progress in following the trail left by whoever had captured Jessie. He watched the brightening ground, and as soon as he could see his surroundings clearly without having to stoop to make out details, Ki picked up the reins of the horses and started moving ahead in a series of wide half-circles, zigzagging back and forth while flicking his eyes from side to side as he searched the area ahead of him.

Much sooner than Ki had feared, he came across the tracks he'd been seeking. The prints were deeper now, but he saw no signs of any that could have been made by Jessie's small boots. A frown formed on Ki's face, and as he advanced, he slowed his pace a bit while widening the area of the arcs in which he was moving.

★

Chapter 13

Jessie had been forced by the blinding bandage to keep her eyes closed for such a long time that they were unaccustomed to the light. When her captor lowered her to the ground and removed the cloth that had covered a good part of her face, the soft sky-glow of the setting sun was bright enough to start her eyes watering, and she had to blink for a moment to clear them.

As soon as she'd winked away the tears that blurred her vision, Jessie started swiveling her head from side to side. After a few moments her vision was totally clear. Now it was possible for her to see that since she and the creature toting her had started moving, they'd left the stump forest. They were in a broad valley that held no trees, but was an expanse of grassed meadowland. She also discovered that she was sitting on the ground a short distance away from a small cabin.

It was, Jessie thought, no great shakes as a building. Its shed roof was canted at an angle because the entire little board structure itself leaned slightly out of perpendicular. The roof shingles curved up at each side, the walls seemed awry, and in many of the unpainted boards long cracks were opening. Jessie looked back at the figure who'd captured her, and for a moment wondered when she'd find out if she'd been taken prisoner by a man or some sort of alien creature.

From the first time Jessie had glimpsed her captor, she'd known that he was big. With her sight restored, she realized that she'd previously had no guidelines to judge his true size. Although Jessie had seen big men before, the creature covered with fur who now stood before her dwarfed them all. She could get no idea of his facial features; they were hidden by the same long, tangled fur that covered his limbs and body. All that she could be sure of was that his head was small in comparison to the width and depth of his shoulders and the bulk of his limbs and torso.

Even after Jessie thought she'd looked him over thoroughly, he did not seem real. His husky arms and legs were the size of small tree trunks. He had huge hands, their backs covered with corkscrewlike curls of short, shaggy tan fur, but it was his feet that made Jessie arch her brows in surprise. They were enormous both in their length and in their spread across his toes.

He gazed at Jessie for only a few moments, then pushed the cabin's door open and picked her up, holding her like a baby cradled in his arms. The entry was both narrow and low; he had to bend forward and angle sideways to carry her inside. An edge of the door frame brushed against one of Jessie's shoulders as he bent forward to go into the cabin, reminding her again of the height and bulk of the creature carrying her.

Once inside, he stepped up to a short, backless bench, little wider than a chair. He leaned forward until his head and shoulders were close to the floor and shrugged his shoulder. At the same time he relaxed the hold he'd maintained almost constantly on Jessie from the moment he'd picked her up.

Jessie interpreted his moves as an invitation for her to slide out of his arms onto the bench. Without stopping to inspect her surroundings, she did so. When she'd settled onto the bench, she twisted around a time or two, trying to find a comfortable position. After a second when she realized that the hard, flat surface of the bench had no comfortable spots, Jessie gave her full attention to her captor.

After closing the door and bolting it, he bent over to examine the bonds that secured her wrists. As his head came close to her eyes, she could see for the first time that his face was covered with a mask crafted from some sort of animal skin. It covered his forehead below his hat and extended to form a huge snoutlike nose above a white beard that cupped his chin. Before she could begin asking any of the dozen or so questions that had been stirring in her mind, he spoke.

"You don't have to worry," he said. His voice was muffled by the mask he had on, but it bore a tone of assurance. He went on, "I'm not going to hurt you. Just stay still and I'm sure that everything will be all right."

"If everything is all right, why do you have to keep me tied up?" she asked.

"Perhaps I will be able to give you more freedom later," he replied. "But that will depend on what you tell me."

"Tell you?" she frowned. "About what?"

"We will talk of that after a while," he said quickly. "First I must start a fire. Soon it will be dark and we will get very cold. After the sun goes, when the wind

147

begins blowing in off the ocean tonight, it will be even colder. Just sit quietly. I won't harm you."

Jessie lay without moving, her eyes flicking over the interior of the little cabin. Her first discovery was that it had no windows. Its interior was murky dark, lit only by the slice of light that came through the open door, and Jessie's second discovery was that it was the only door that broke the cabin's walls. By this time her eyes had adjusted to the dimness of the interior, and she began taking stock of her new surroundings. She ignored her captor, who still stood quietly and motionless beside the bed.

It was a small room, crowded by even the few bits of furniture it contained. Jessie needed very little time to scan the place; she completed her inspection with three or four quick flicks of her eyes. The cabin held a narrow single bed, a straight chair with a low footstool in front of it, a small potbellied stove, and a one-legged shelf. The shelf jutted from the wall near the stove and extended into the room.

Jessie realized that the shelf was a substitute for a table, and turned her attention to the remainder of the cramped chamber. Pegs had been driven into the wall on the opposite side of the room, beside the narrow bed. From them hung a scanty array of garments: a shirt or two and a set of faded red wool long johns, two or three pairs of blue jeans and a couple of thick winter jackets. The other walls were bare.

Jessie had been puzzled by her treatment since the big creature had grabbed her and started to run from the stump-filled area. Now the attention she was receiving only increased her perplexity. Her efficient survey of the cabin's interior had required only a few moments. She turned back to the huge hairy form of the man

148

disguised as a creature; he still stood just inside the door, watching her.

"You've already proved that you're human and that you can talk," she said. "And I'm also sure that you can understand what I'm saying to you. I'd like to have you answer me."

Jessie's words brought no more response from her captor than had her earlier requests. He had moved to the stove and was laying small sticks of wood onto the coals that had been glowing a soft dying red when he opened the door of the firebox. The sticks caught very quickly; small flames were running along their length before the man closed the door. He turned back, glanced at Jessie, then pulled the stool up closer to the bed before settling down on it.

After he'd shifted around on the stool for a moment, still without uttering a word, Jessie decided to try starting the conversation she'd suggested. She said, "Please tell me who you are and why you've brought me here. I'm also very curious about that fur outfit you've put on to make you look like an animal."

"It may be that I have the mind of an animal," he replied after a pause that lasted so long Jessie had begun to fear he would not respond to her request. Then he shook his head as he went on. "No. I would never admit to that."

"And I wouldn't blame you," Jessie said assuringly. "But I don't believe you can blame me for wondering why you choose to go around the Mendocino countryside disguised as an animal."

"Of course you'd wonder," he answered. "My name is Daniel Brady. And the reason I'm dressed as I am now is quite easy to explain. I'm paid to wear these skins and the huge shoes I have on, and to walk through the stump forest as I do. People call me the Mendocino Monster."

Jessie had managed to keep her features expressionless in spite of the sudden affirmation of her deductions. She decided now that the man who'd captured her must have a reason for both her abduction and the revelation he'd just made. Realizing at once that since he'd shown no hesitance in confessing to his identity, he must certainly be prepared tell her more, she knew she had to keep him talking.

"I've certainly heard about the Mendocino Monster. You mean somebody's paying you to wear that outfit you've got on?" Jessie frowned. "And go around frightening people?"

"Of course. Otherwise, I'd have no reason to wear it. This is the only way I have to earn the money I need to buy food."

As he spoke, Brady was pulling off one of the thick fur-backed gloves that covered his hands and arms almost to his elbows. He extended his bared arm toward Jessie, and she saw that only the short stubs of two fingers and a part of his thumb remained on his hand.

"A logging saw took my fingers off a long time ago," he went on. "And my other hand's only a little bit better than this one. My feet were crushed so that I must be careful when I walk. I wear these long gloves because I don't like to show my infirmities to everyone, Miss Starbuck."

"If you stay by yourself in the woods here, how is it that you know my name?" Jessie frowned.

"I was told to be watching for you. But your name's not strange to me, Miss Starbuck. A good long time back, I worked for your father."

Jessie's jaw dropped, and she stared at him for a

150

moment before asking, "Where was it you worked for Alex? And when?"

"It was in Alaska," Brady replied. "When your father was opening the great timber stand on Forty Mile Creek. And it was there that I played the fool with a felling saw and—Well, you can see what's left of my hands."

"But Alex always took care of any of his men who got hurt on one of his jobs!" Jessie protested.

"He took care of me, very good care. If I hadn't been foolish enough to gamble on one of Soapy Smith's rigged wheels, I'd still be well off. But there's not much a man who doesn't have good hands can do, so I work at any kind of job I can find. That's why I'm working for Vance Harper now."

"Then that's why you brought me here!" Jessie exclaimed. "You're going to turn me over to Harper?"

"That's not what I said," Brady protested. "Working for Vance Harper's not what I'd choose to do, but there are a lot of times when I don't have any choice but to take whatever kind of job that comes my way."

"But why would Harper want you to go around frightening people here in Mendocino?" Jessie asked, her frown deepening.

"There are always timber thieves working somewhere in these stands, Miss Starbuck," Brady answered. "And you saw the stump forest, I'm sure."

"Yes, of course, and it's something I'd never seen before. Ki and I sheltered in it last night. But there certainly aren't any harvestable stands in it. If there'd been any, I'm sure we'd have seen them." The frown was growing on Jessie's face as she went on. "All that forest has in it are stumps. There aren't any trees in it, and from what I could see it'll be years before it will be a forest of trees big enough to have any value."

"Not so," Brady replied. "It will be a very short time. Within a very few years, five, perhaps as many as seven, those small, whippy shoots will be a huge forest of small pine trees."

"But they'll still be too small to make lumber!" Jessie frowned. "Why would anyone want them?"

"Oh, the trees that'll grow out of those stumps won't touch big mature pines for size," Brady agreed. "But they'll be immensely valuable because of their fine, clear grain and because they're easy for the factories to work with. Of course the shoots will still have to grow a great deal before they're ready to go to market, but already Harper has had the big furniture factories back east bidding for them."

"But those stumps and saplings aren't on Harper's land!" Jessie protested. "Even if that stand of pines isn't ready to be cut yet, it's still Starbuck property!"

"I'm afraid that very few people have respect for property lines here on the Mendocino coast. Why do you think that Harper had his hired gunmen kidnap you?"

"Oh, he made no secret of what he wanted," Jessie replied. "And I hadn't learned then how much money can be made from that forest of stumps."

"Well, now that you know, what do you propose to do about him stealing from you?"

"I'll stop him, of course," she said, almost before Brady had finished speaking. "I'm not sure how, but I'll work out a way to protect my property."

"If you're thinking about stopping Harper by taking him to the law, you might as well give up the idea, Miss Starbuck," Brady told her. His voice was sober. "He's got every judge in this part of the country folded up like a handkerchief and tucked away in his pocket.

As far as the Mendocino country's concerned, Harper's the boss."

"That's a situation I've run into more times than I care to remember," Jessie said levelly. "And I've learned that there are a number of ways to change unpopular situations such as the one you've told me about. I'm sure there are some people left here who're tired of having a self-appointed boss."

"Plenty. You can count me among them," he assured her. "I'll join into whatever you get started, and I know a number of others who will, too."

"We'll talk about it more, later on," Jessie said. "Right now I'm more interested in getting a bite of something to eat, if such a thing is possible."

Ki's progress had been slow. Jessie's horse had been troublesome to lead, and both it and his own mount were tiring. As the light began to go, he'd found that keeping to the indistinct trail he'd been following was more and more difficult. He'd finally dismounted and was now leading both horses.

He'd almost worked his way through the stand of stumps now, and between the small openings in the foliage he could glimpse clear, high-grassed land ahead. A narrow shimmer of haze showed as an almost invisible streak in the sky. Ki turned and started toward it.

Now that he had a goal in sight, Ki moved at a faster pace. When his long, quick strides had brought him near the cabin, he stopped for a moment and hunkered down to make a closer, quick inspection of the little structure. He saw no one stirring. Most importantly, there were no windows in either of the walls that were visible from where he squatted.

Once satisfied that there was little or no danger that he would be seen, Ki looked around in search of a place to leave the horses. A rock outcrop broke the earth a short distance away. He led the animals to the most convenient of the protruding stones and piled two heavy flat rocks on their reins, then stepped up to Jessie's mount and reached for the rifle in its saddle scabbard. He'd started to draw the weapon when he realized that it would be more hindrance than help to him, and that it was unlikely to be used by Jessie. Letting the weapon slide back into its holster, he turned and started toward the cabin.

He took long strides and wove from side to side to make sure that he would see anyone coming from behind the little structure.

He'd still seen no evidence that it was occupied regularly or that there was anybody inside it at the present moment. However, the footprints that had led him to it indicated that Jessie and her captor must be in the weatherbeaten little building. Ki continued his silent, cautious approach toward the cabin's door.

★

Chapter 14

"I'm afraid this isn't a very appealing meal," Brady said to Jessie, his voice apologetic. "I'm used to just scraping up a bite from whatever's at hand, but I'm sure your regular suppers are something more than fried salt-pork and cheese with hard ship's biscuits."

"I've gotten along quite well with much less for supper than we're having now," Jessie assured him. "And with food that was a good deal less appetizing, as well."

Jessie was sitting in the room's one chair and Brady on the foot of the tousled bed. They faced each other across the wide plank that extended from the wall near the foot of the bed. Brady had insisted on doing the culinary chores, and Jessie had made no objection. Their supper also included very skimpy servings of a stew left over from one of Brady's earlier meals. The meat was toughly stringy and the potatoes softly mushy, but Jessie was attacking her food with a great deal of gusto.

They ate without trying to make conversation. Half the food on their plates had been consumed when they heard the distant thudding of horses' hooves. Brady looked up from his plate, a frown on his face.

"I'd say that we've got some guests on the way, Miss Starbuck," he said. "I hope it's not somebody beholden to Vance Harper that's tracked us here."

"If someone has been tracking us, I hope it's Ki," she told Brady. "Because if it is him, he'll have our horses, and I won't waste any time in getting back to Mendocino City. You might be interested to know I've decided that the first thing I intend to do there is to swear out an arrest warrant for Vance Harper."

Brady had gotten to his feet by this time and was heading for the door. Jessie followed him. When he opened the door, the hoofbeats were louder than they had been but no rider was in sight. Brady stepped outside, Jessie a pace or two behind him. The full moon had come up now, and its light was making their surroundings almost as bright as day. Jessie dodged back quickly when a rifle cracked in the distance and its slug tore into the cabin's wall, only a few inches from her head.

Ki heard the shot and the high-pitched singing of the slug that whistled above his head a split-second before he'd reached the door that Brady was opening. He lurched forward and lay motionless, twisting his head as he tried to find the location from which the rifle shot had come.

Another shot sounded, but by this time both Brady and Ki were on the ground, staring at each other across the few feet of space that separated them.

Then Jessie spoke from the cabin, "Ki! You'll never know how glad I am to see you! I'd be even gladder if you brought my rifle with you. Did you?"

"No," Ki replied. His voice was calmly level. "But I didn't know we were going need to defend ourselves."

156

"Neither did I," Brady put in. "I guess you'd be the Ki that Jessie mentioned to me a while ago?"

"Yes, I am," Ki replied. "But I didn't have any way to know I was going to run into a gunfight." Looking up at Jessie, who was crouched down just inside the cabin's opened door, he asked, "You do have your Colt, don't you?"

"Of course. But I don't have any shells except the five in the cylinder. My spare ammunition's in my saddlebags."

"What caliber pistol are you talking about, a .44 or a .45?" Brady broke in to ask. "I've got a box of .44s inside."

"My Colt's a .45," Jessie told him. "But I appreciate your offer. And Ki has his own weapons, not guns."

"Don't worry about about me," Ki said. "As Jessie knows, my own silent weapons are very satisfactory. But in our situation, I suggest that instead of going out to seek a fight, we let the fight come to us. I think the best thing we can do is hole up right here where we are."

"Neither Daniel nor I will argue about that, Ki," Jessie said. She turned to Brady with a questioning look.

"You won't get an argument out of me," he said. "And you two'll sure be welcome. It'll do me good to feel like I've got somebody on my side for a change. I just wish we had a better place to hole up in."

"From the sound of those rifle shots, I'd say that whoever's doing the shooting is out of range for my Colt right now," Jessie said. "And I'll certainly wait until he gets closer before I try to use it."

"That's not going to be much help as long as we're pinned down by his rifle," Brady commented. "Right now all we know is that somebody's after our hides, but we still don't know who it it is."

"I'd be surprised if Vance Harper didn't have a hand in it," Jessie went on. "Ki and I saw him kill two of his outlaws, and the only reason he had was that he was afraid they'd talk about him hiring them to kidnap me. I'm sure that whoever those men are out there, Harper's behind them."

Though only a few seconds had passed during the exchange between Jessie and Ki and Brady, their brief interval of inactivity had lasted long enough to give their assailants time to move closer. The next shot that sounded sent a slug crashing through the flimsy wall and whistling across the cabin to strike the opposite wall, where it hit with a subdued thunk and dropped to the floor.

"We're not going to win this fight by staying cooped up in here like a bunch of penned chickens," Jessie said. She turned to Ki and asked, "How far away are our horses?"

"Not very far," he replied. "I can get to them without a great deal of risk, if that's what you're asking."

Jessie nodded abstractedly; then she went on, "It's not just getting to them. It's getting them here alive and ready to ride. And I want my rifle, too."

"Are you sure it's Harper who's sniping at us?"

"Who else could it be?" she asked quickly. "I'm his target, Ki. He wants that big stand of new pines and it looks like he's willing to kill to get them."

"That certainly makes sense." Ki nodded. Then he went on, "It won't be much of a trick to get the horses here from the place where I left them. There's only a short stretch of open country to cross getting them here."

Jessie went on thoughtfully, "Right now, it's a case of fight or run, and I know you're not inclined to run any more than I am, Ki."

"I'll go get them, then," Ki nodded.

"Which way will you be coming from?" Jessie asked him.

"I'll stay in the arroyos as much as I can," Ki told her. "And coming back I'll cut a straight line down the slope to the cabin here."

Brady had been listening while Jessie and Ki talked. Now he said, "I'll get out what rifle ammunition I've got in my little cache, and I'm sure that you'll see to Jessie's rifle having a full load."

"It has," Jessie broke in. "And I'm sure all three of us will know what to do after we get the horses here."

Ki nodded and started for the door. He dropped to a belly crawl as he reached it and disappeared over the threshold.

Crouched beside the doorjamb, Jessie and Brady watched Ki as he began a *ninja*-crawl away from the cabin, cutting a long angle up the slope toward the spot where he'd left the horses. Ki had covered only a short distance before he seemed to disappear as he wriggled his way forward.

"I don't suppose we have much to do but wait," Jessie said to her companion. "And be ready to move when Ki gets back."

"Being ready means at least a skeleton plan," he replied. "And I'm not as good at this kind of thing as I used to be. But even if I don't have all my fingers, I can still use a rifle pretty well with my stubs."

"What sort of plan?" Jessie frowned. "Ki and I have been in this sort of corner before, and we know what to do."

"But I don't know your style yet," Brady pointed out.

"Maybe we've stayed alive because we don't have any set style," she answered. "We'll just spread out and start

159

toward Vance Harper and whoever's with him out there trying to kill us. And as you already know, we don't feel like waiting for them to fire the first shots."

They fell silent then, watching the the long moonlight-brightened slope between the cabin and the riverbed, waiting for Ki to appear.

Without pausing, Ki had run at a dogtrot to reach the spot where he'd tethered the two horses. He went first to Jessie's mount and checked on the condition of her rifle. It was fully loaded. Replacing the weapon in its saddle scabbard, he took the animal's reins. Mounting his own horse, Ki nudged it ahead, keeping to the high ground of the long slope down to the cabin.

Now and then Ki stood up in his stirrups to scan the terrain, but he'd seen no signs of Harper's men when he came in sight of the cabin. He'd settled back to the saddle and was reining his horse toward his destination when another rifle shot barked and the bullet cut the air only inches above his head. Ki kicked his horse's flanks and the animal leaped ahead.

Had Ki not been an expert horseman, he'd have been pulled from the saddle, but he'd dropped both hands to the saddle horn and grasped it as his kicks landed. Ki's mount was almost dragging the led horse as they rushed down the long slant. The unseen rifleman fired again, and dust spurted only a short distance in front of Ki's mount. He was quick with the reins and managed to turn the horse aside and head in a different direction almost before the puff of dust had settled.

When the next shot sounded, Ki glimpsed a spurt of muzzle flash from the vicinity of the cabin. He recognized it as a sign that Brady was joining the fight now, and made no effort to rein in the headlong rush the horses were making toward the cabin.

Two more shots from the cabin's attackers broke the air before Ki reached his goal, but both missed. Jessie and Brady were waiting to mount when Ki reined in.

"My bet is that Harper and his crew are trying to circle us," Jessie said as she swung into the saddle and took the reins Ki handed her. "But instead of waiting for them to find us, I'd say we'll be better off if we go after them."

They saw no red flash of gunfire, but from somewhere on the forested downslope beyond the cabin a rifle cracked and dust spurted just short of the hooves of Jessie's horse. It stomped but did not rear.

"That shot was from those bushes, there at the end of the slope," Brady said. "Do we fight, or do we run?"

"There's only one way to win," Jessie replied quickly. "We fight. Head toward the place where that shot came from."

She was turning her mount as she spoke. Ki and Brady followed her as she galloped, and the three had almost reached the dark mass of the stump forest before another shot sounded from the blackness of the shaded area ahead. Its muzzle blast lasted for only the fraction of a second, but Jessie and Ki could see very plainly the outlined figure of a man with a shouldered rifle against the dark sprawl of the stump forest.

Before Jessie could bring up her own weapon, the rifleman fired again. Brady's mount reared as it loosed a shrill neigh. It began tottering and starting to collapse.

"You two go on!" Brady called. "I'll catch up with you as soon as I can!"

Jessie thunked her heels into the sides of her horse, and Ki toed his own mount to bring it abreast of Jessie's.

161

"Did you see the muzzle flash?" Ki asked after he'd settled down on the horse's rump.

"That's where we're heading now!" Jessie replied. "And I'm sure Brady is, too, even if we can't see him in the dark."

"Can we really be sure it's Harper ahead?"

"Who else would it be? I think he's too smart to hire anybody he can't dispose of like he did those two men who brought me to him," Jessie said.

Ki could not argue against her logic. He looked over Jessie's shoulder at the line of the stump forest that loomed ahead of them in a dark, forbidding mass.

"There, Ki!" Jessie exclaimed suddenly. "To the right of us!"

Ki turned his eyes in the direction she'd mentioned. He saw a man solidly outlined in black against the dappled background of the stump forest. The black silhouette was crossed by the equally dark outline of the rifle he was shouldering.

Ki was slipping a *shuriken* from its case while Jessie struggled with the stock of her rifle. His moves were a bit faster than Jessie's. The *shuriken* caught the skyglow as it whirled to its mark. A moment after it had vanished into the darkness at the edge of the foliage, Jessie fired. The muzzle blast was bright enough to illuminate the crumpling figure of the man who'd been trying to shoulder his rifle, and there was no mistaking his identity.

"Vance Harper!" Jessie exclaimed.

"Yes, there's no question about that," Ki agreed.

"And if you need another guarantee, I'll give it to you," Brady said as his shadowy figure come into their limited arc of vision. "I saw him pretty close up. Fact is, I was about ready to throw down on him when one of you beat me to it."

162

Jessie loosed a sigh as she settled back into the saddle. Then she said, "I suppose that means our problem here is solved, Ki. Except for the close look we still need to give to the mill." Turning to Brady, she went on, "I have an idea that might interest you. Instead of being the Mendocino Monster, how would you feel about going to work at the Starbuck Mill here?"

"But how would I be any use to you?" Brady asked, holding out his mangled hands. "I can't use these to write with, or do anything but—"

"I don't want to hire your hands," Jessie broke in. "I want to hire your brain, to think and to help my young manager to think. I'm sure all three of us will benefit. You think about it, and we'll discuss it later. In the meantime, Ki and I will be looking over the mill and the forests without having to keep our eyes peeled for the Mendocino Monster."

THE HORSEMEN

by Gary McCarthy

The Ballous were the finest horsemen in the South, a Tennessee family famous for the training and breeding of glorious Thoroughbreds. When the Civil War devastated their home and their lives, they headed West—into the heart of Indian territory. As horsemen, they triumphed. As a family, they endured. But as pioneers in a new land, they faced unimaginable hardship, danger, and ruthless enemies. . . .

Turn the page for a preview of this exciting new western series . . .

The Horsemen

Now available from Diamond Books!

November 24, 1863—Just east of Chattanooga, Tennessee

The chestnut stallion's head snapped up very suddenly. Its nostrils quivered, then flared, testing the wind, tasting the approach of unseen danger. Old Justin Ballou's watchful eye caught the stallion's motion and he also froze, senses focused. For several long moments, man and stallion remained motionless, and then Justin Ballou opened the gate to the paddock and limped toward the tall Thoroughbred. He reached up and his huge, blue-veined hand stroked the stallion's muzzle. "What is it, High Man?" he asked softly. "What now, my friend?"

In answer, the chestnut dipped its head several times and stamped its feet with increasing nervousness. Justin began to speak soothingly to the stallion, his deep, resonant voice flowing like a mystical incantation. Almost at once, the stallion grew calm. After a few minutes, Justin said, as if to an old and very dear

169

friend, "Is it one of General Grant's Union patrols this time, High Man? Have they come to take what little I have left? If so, I will gladly fight them to the death."

The stallion shook its head, rolled its eyes, and snorted as if it could smell Yankee blood. Justin's thick fingers scratched a special place behind the stallion's ear. The chestnut lowered its head to nuzzle the man's chest.

"Don't worry. It's probably another Confederate patrol," Justin said thoughtfully. "But what can they want this time? I have already given them three fine sons and most of your offspring. There is so little left to give—but they know that! Surely they can see my empty stalls and paddocks."

Justin turned toward the road leading past his neat, whitewashed fences that sectioned and cross-sectioned his famous Tennessee horse ranch, known throughout the South as Wildwood Farm. The paddocks were empty and silent. This cold autumn day, there were proud mares with their colts, and prancing fillies blessed the old man's vision and gave him the joy he'd known for so many years. It was the war—this damned killing Civil War. "No more!" Justin cried. "You'll have no more of my fine horses or sons!"

The stallion spun and galloped away. High Man was seventeen years old, long past his prime, but he and a few other Ballou-bred stallions still sired the fastest and handsomest horses in the South. Just watching the chestnut run made Justin feel a little better. High Man was a living testimony to the extraordinarily fine care he'd received all these years at Wildwood Farms. No one would believe that at his ripe age he could still run and kick his heels up like a three-year-old colt.

The stallion ran with such fluid grace that he seemed

to float across the earth. When the Thoroughbred reached the far end of the paddock, it skidded to a sliding stop, chest banging hard against the fence. It spun around, snorted, and shook its head for an expected shout of approval.

But not this day. Instead, Justin made himself leave the paddock, chin up, stride halting but resolute. He could hear thunder growing louder. Could it be the sound of cannon from as far away as the heights that General Bragg and his Rebel army now held in wait of the Union army's expected assault? No, the distance was too great even to carry the roar of heavy artillery. That told Justin that his initial hunch was correct and the sound growing in his ears had to be racing hoofbeats.

But were they enemy or friend? Blue coat or gray? Justin planted his big work boots solidly in the dust of the country road; either way, he would meet them.

"Father!"

He recognized his fourteen-year-old daughter's voice and ignored it, wanting Dixie to stay inside their mansion. Justin drew a pepperbox pistol from his waistband. If this actually was a dreaded Union cavalry patrol, then someone was going to die this afternoon. A man could only be pushed so far and then he had to fight.

"Father!" Dixie's voice was louder now, more strident. "Father!"

Justin reluctantly twisted about to see his daughter and her older brother, Houston, running toward him. Both had guns clenched in their fists.

"Who is it!" Houston gasped, reaching Justin first and trying to catch his wind.

Justin did not dignify the stupid question with an answer. In a very few minutes, they would know. "Dixie, go back to the house."

"Please, I . . . I just can't!"

"Dixie! Do as Father says," Houston stormed. "This is no time for arguing. Go to the house!"

Dixie's black eyes sparked. She stood her ground. Houston was twenty-one and a man full grown, but he was still just her big brother. "I'm staying."

Houston's face darkened with anger and his knuckles whitened as he clutched the gun in his fist. "Dammit, you heard . . ."

"Quiet, the both of you!" Justin commanded. "Here they come."

A moment later a dust-shrouded patrol lifted from the earth to come galloping up the road.

"It's *our* boys," Dixie yelped with relief. "It's a Reb patrol!"

"Yeah," Houston said, taking an involuntary step forward, "but they been shot up all to hell!"

Justin slipped his gun back into his waistband and was seized by a flash of dizziness. Dixie moved close, steadying him until the spell passed a moment later. "You all right?"

Justin nodded. He did not know what was causing the dizziness, but the spells seemed to come often these days. No doubt, it was the war. This damned war that the South was steadily losing. And the death of two of his five strapping sons and . . .

Houston had stepped out in front and now he turned to shout, "Mason is riding with them!"

Justin's legs became solid and strong again. Mason was the middle son, the short, serious one that wanted to go into medicine and who read volumes of poetry despite the teasing from his brothers.

Dixie slipped her gun into the pocket of the loose-fitting pants she insisted on wearing around the horses.

172

She glanced up at her father and said, "Mason will be hungry and so will the others. They'll need food and bandaging."

"They'll have both," Justin declared without hesitation, "but no more of my Thoroughbreds!"

"No more," Dixie vowed. "Mason will understand."

"Yeah," Houston said, coming back to stand by his father, "but the trouble is, he isn't in charge. That's a captain he's riding alongside."

Justin was about to speak, but from the corner of his eyes, saw a movement. He twisted, hand instinctively lifting the pepperbox because these woods were crawling with both Union and Confederate deserters, men often half-crazy with fear and hunger.

"Pa, don't you dare shoot me!" Rufus "Ruff" Ballou called, trying to force a smile as he moved forward, long and loose limbed with his rifle swinging at his side.

"Ruff, what the hell you doing hiding in those trees!" Houston demanded, for he too had been startled enough to raise his gun.

If Ruff noticed the heat in his older brother's voice, he chose to ignore it.

"Hell, Houston, I was just hanging back a little to make sure these were friendly visitors."

"It's Mason," Justin said, turning back to the patrol. "And from the looks of these boys, things are going from bad to worse."

There were just six men in the patrol, two officers and four enlisted. One of the enlisted was bent over nearly double with pain, a blossom of red spreading across his left shoulder. Two others were riding double on a runty sorrel.

"That sorrel is gonna drop if it don't get feed and rest," Ruff observed, his voice hardening with disapproval.

"All of their mounts look like they've been chased to hell and back without being fed or watered," Justin stated. "We'll make sure they're watered and grained before these boys leave."

The Ballous nodded. It never occurred to any of them that a horse should ever leave their farm in worse shape than when it had arrived. The welfare of livestock just naturally came first—even over their own physical needs.

Justin stepped forward and raised his hand in greeting. Deciding that none of the horses were in desperate circumstances, he fixed his attention on Mason. He was shocked. Mason was a big man, like his father and brothers, but now he appeared withered—all ridges and angles. His cap was missing and his black hair was wild and unkept. His cheeks were hollow, and the sleeve of his right arm had been cut away, and now his arm was wrapped in a dirty bandage. The loose, sloppy way he sat his horse told Justin more eloquently than words how weak and weary Mason had become after just eight months of fighting the armies of the North.

The patrol slowed to a trot, then a walk, and Justin saw the captain turn to speak to Mason. Justin couldn't hear the words, but he could see by the senior officer's expression that the man was angry and upset. Mason rode trancelike, eyes fixed on his family, lips a thin, hard slash instead of the expected smile of greeting.

Mason drew his horse to a standstill before his father and brothers. Up close, his appearance was even more shocking.

"Mason?" Justin whispered when his son said nothing. "Mason, are you all right?"

Mason blinked. Shook himself. "Father. Houston. Ruff. Dixie. You're all looking well. How are the horses?"

"What we got left are fine," Justin said cautiously. "Only a few on the place even fit to run. Sold all the fillies and colts last fall. But you knew that."

"You did the right thing to keep Houston and Ruff out of this," Mason said.

Houston and Ruff took a sudden interest in the dirt under their feet. The two youngest Ballou brothers had desperately wanted to join the Confederate army, but Justin had demanded that they remain at Wildwood Farm, where they could help carry on the family business of raising Thoroughbreds. Only now, instead of racetracks and cheering bettors, the Ballou horses swiftly carried messages between the generals of the Confederate armies. Many times the delivery of a vital message depended on horses with pure blazing speed.

"Lieutenant," the captain said, clearing his throat loudly, "I think this chatter has gone on quite long enough. Introduce me."

Mason flushed with humiliation. "Father, allow me to introduce Captain Denton."

Justin had already sized up the captain, and what he saw did not please him. Denton was a lean, straight-backed man. He rode as if he had a rod up his ass and he looked like a mannequin glued to the saddle. He was an insult to the fine tradition of Southern cavalry officers.

"Captain," Justin said without warmth, "if you'll order your patrol to dismount, we'll take care of your wounded and these horses."

"Private Wilson can't ride any farther," Denton said. "And there isn't time for rest."

"But you *have* to," Justin argued. "These horses are—"

"Finished," Denton said. "We must have replacements;

that's why we are here, Mr. Ballou."

Justin paled ever so slightly. "Hate to tell you this, Captain, but I'm afraid you're going to be disappointed. I've already given all the horses I can to the Confederacy—sons, too."

Denton wasn't listening. His eyes swept across the paddock.

"What about *that* one," he said, pointing toward High Man. "He looks to be in fine condition."

"He's past his racing prime," Houston argued. "He's our foundation sire now and is used strictly for breeding."

"Strictly for breeding?" Denton said cryptically. "Mr. Ballou, there is not a male creature on this earth who would not like to—"

"Watch your tongue, sir!" Justin stormed. "My daughter's honor will not be compromised!"

Captain Denton's eyes jerked sideways to Dixie and he blushed. Obviously, he had not realized Dixie was a girl with her baggy pants and a felt slouch hat pulled down close to her eyebrows. And a Navy Colt hanging from her fist.

"My sincere apologies." The captain dismissed her and his eyes came to rest on the barns. "You've got horses in those stalls?"

"Yes, but—"

"I'd like to see them," Denton said, spurring his own flagging mount forward.

Ruff grabbed his bit. "Hold up there, Captain, you haven't been invited."

"And since when does an officer of the Confederacy need to beg permission for horses so that *your* countrymen, as well as mine, can live according to our own laws!"

"*I'm* the law on this place," Justin thundered. "And my mares are in foal. They're not going to war, Captain. Neither they nor the last of my stallions are going to be chopped to pieces on some battlefield or have their legs ruined while trying to pull supply wagons. These are *Thoroughbred* horses, sir! Horses bred to race."

"The race," Denton said through clenched teeth, "is to see if we can bring relief to our men who are, this very moment, fighting and dying at Lookout Mountain and Missionary Ridge."

Denton's voice shook with passion. "The plundering armies of General Ulysses Grant, General George Thomas, and his Army of the Cumberland are attacking our soldiers right now, and God help me if I've ever seen such slaughter! Our boys are dying, Mr. Ballou! Dying for the right to determine the South's great destiny. We—not you and your piddling horses—are making the ultimate sacrifices! But maybe your attitude has a lot to do with why you married a Cherokee Indian woman."

Something snapped behind Justin Ballou's obsidian eyes. He saw the faces of his two oldest sons, one reported to have been blown to pieces by a Union battery in the battle of Bull Run and the other trampled to death in a bloody charge at Shiloh. Their proud mother's Cherokee blood had made them the first in battle and the first in death.

Justin lunged, liver-spotted hands reaching upward. Too late Captain Denton saw murder in the old man's eyes. He tried to rein his horse off, but Justin's fingers clamped on his coat and his belt. With a tremendous heave, Denton was torn from his saddle and hurled to the ground. Justin growled like a huge dog as his fingers crushed the breath out of Denton's life.

He would have broken the Confederate captain's neck

if his sons had not broken his stranglehold. Two of the mounted soldiers reached for their pistols, but Ruff's own rifle made them freeze and then slowly raise their hands.

"Pa!" Mason shouted, pulling Justin off the nearly unconscious officer. "Pa, stop it!"

As suddenly as it had flared, Justin's anger ended, and he had to be helped to his feet. He glared down at the wheezing cavalry officer and his voice trembled when he said, "Captain Denton, I don't know how the hell you managed to get a commission in Jeff Davis's army, but I do know this: lecture me about sacrifice for the South again and I will break your fool neck! Do you hear me!"

The captain's eyes mirrored raw animal fear. "Lieutenant Ballou," he choked at Mason, "I *order* you in the name of the Army of the Confederacy to confiscate fresh horses!"

"Go to hell."

"I'll have you court-martialed and shot for insubordination!"

Houston drew his pistol and aimed it at Denton's forehead. "Maybe you'd better change your tune, Captain."

"No!"

Justin surprised them all by coming to Denton's defense. "If you shoot him—no matter how much he deserves to be shot—our family will be judged traitors."

"But . . ."

"Put the gun away," Justin ordered wearily. "I'll give him fresh horses."

"Pa!" Ruff cried. "What are you going to give to him? Our mares?"

"Yes, but not all of them. Just the youngest and the

178

strongest. And those matched three-year-old stallions you and Houston are training."

"But, Pa," Ruff protested, "they're just green broke."

"I know, but this will season them in a hurry," Justin said levelly. "Besides, there's no choice. High Man leaves Wildwood Farm over my dead body."

"Yes, sir," Ruff said, knowing his father was not running a bluff.

Dixie turned away in anger and started toward the house. "I'll see we get food cooking for the soldiers and some fresh bandages for Private Wilson."

A moment later, Ruff stepped over beside the wounded soldier. "Here, let me give you a hand down. We'll go up to the house and take a look at that shoulder."

Wilson tried to show his appreciation as both Ruff and Houston helped him to dismount. "Much obliged," he whispered. "Sorry to be of trouble."

Mason looked to his father. "Sir, I'll take responsibility for your horses."

"How can you do that?" Houston demanded of his brother. "These three-year-old stallions and our mares will go crazy amid all that cannon and rifle fire. No one but us can control them. It would be—"

"Then you and Ruff need to come on back with us," Mason said.

"No!" Justin raged. "I paid for their replacements! I've got the papers saying that they can't be drafted or taken into the Confederate army."

"Maybe not," Mason said, "but they can volunteer to help us save lives up on the mountains where General Bragg is in danger of being overrun, and where our boys are dying for lack of medical attention."

"No!" Justin choked. "I've given too much already!"

"Pa, we won't fight. We'll just go to handle the

179

horses." Ruff placed his hand on his father's shoulder. "No fighting," he pledged, looking past his father at the road leading toward Chattanooga and the battlefields. "I swear it."

Justin shook his head, not believing a word of it. His eyes shifted from Mason to Houston and finally settled on Ruff. "You boys are *fighters*! Oh, I expect you'll even try to do as you promised, but you won't be able to once you smell gunpowder and death. You'll fight and get yourselves killed, just like Micha and John."

Mason shook his head vigorously. "Pa, I swear that once the horses are delivered and hitched to those ambulances and supply wagons, I'll send Houston and Ruff back to you. All right?"

After a long moment, Justin finally managed to nod his head. "Come along," he said to no one in particular, "we'll get our Thoroughbreds ready."

But Captain Denton's thin lips twisted in anger. "I want a *dozen* horses! Not one less will do. And I still want that big chestnut stallion in that paddock for my personal mount."

Houston scoffed with derision, "Captain, I've seen some fools in my short lifetime, but none as big as you."

"At least," Denton choked, "my daddy didn't buy my way out of the fighting."

Houston's face twisted with fury and his hand went for the Army Colt strapped to his hip. It was all that Ruff could do to keep his older brother from gunning down the ignorant cavalry officer.

"You *are* a fool," Ruff gritted at the captain when he'd calmed Houston down. "And if you should be lucky enough to survive this war, you'd better pray that you never come across me or any of my family."

Denton wanted to say something. His mouth worked but Ruff's eyes told him he wouldn't live long enough to finish even a single sentence, so the captain just clamped his mouth shut and spun away in a trembling rage.

A special offer for people who enjoy reading the best Westerns published today.

WESTERNS!

NO OBLIGATION

Mail the coupon below

To start your subscription and receive 2 FREE WESTERNS, fill out the coupon below and mail it today. We'll send your first shipment which includes 2 FREE BOOKS as soon as we receive it.